Sins of thy Mother Part 2
-A Novel Written by-
Niki Jilvontae

Copyright © 2015 by *True Glory Publications*
Published by True Glory Publications LLC
Join our Mailing list by texting TrueGlory at 95577
Facebook: Author Niki Jilvontae

This novel is a work of fiction. Any resemblances to actual events, real people, living or dead, organizations, establishments or locales are products of the author's imagination. Other names, characters, places, and incidents are used fictitiously.

Cover Design: Michael Horne
Editor: Kylar Bradshaw

Acknowledgments

First, praises to the Most High for this gift and the ability to share it with the world. I'd also like to thank EVERYONE who supports me and believes in me. You all don't understand how much your love means to me. Love you all from the bottom of my heart!

Dedication

I dedicate this book to the son I lost.... I will never forget you my king. You are forever in my heart C.J. 09/11/2001 Mommy loves you!

Table of Contents

Sins Of Thy Mother Part 2

By Niki Jilvontae

Chapter 1

"Tisha, my baby. Mama came to get y'all...everything is gonna be okay now!" Denise said as I glanced at her in utter disbelief.

I could barely breathe let alone believe my eyes as I watched the woman in my nightmares, my mother sit at the island next to my stunned foster mother Tania and another lady who had to be from the courts, smiling at me. I felt light headed as I glared at her and she sat there with her dingy, peach business suit on, her hair pulled into a tight bun, and so much makeup on she resembled a cracked out clown. I could tell that Denise was high as a kite on prescription pills instead of her normal heroin, crack, weed, alcohol mixture because she was a lot calmer and way more focused than she normally was.

Like the true psychopath junky that she was, my mother reserved prescription pills like her bipolar meds mixed with 30 mg Oxycodone for those special occasions, when she had to *wow the judges* as she called it. Any time she had to face the authorities, she would pop a handful of happy pills and then put on her best performance. As I walked into the room, I could tell Denise was up to her old tricks. The way my foster mother was begging me to forgive her with her eyes said it all. I knew right then that Denise had won the best actress award again. She had obviously convinced the courts well enough to get us back, so once again we were being returned to her world, our nightmare. I could do nothing but bite my bottom lip and clench my fists as tears fell from my eyes and I watched as my world was ripped apart.

"Tisha, I'm sorry, there's nothing we can do. This is Mrs. Lee and she is a representative from the court, who works with Child Protection Services. She says that your mother's rights were never taken and she filed the appropriate papers to get you all back. I'm so sorry, Shartisha." Tania said as she got up and walked towards me and I ran into her arms.

I balled like a baby as my foster mother of a few months hugged me with more love than Denise had shown me in my entire 17 years of life. I felt numb and once again shattered as my foster siblings Krista, Jewel, and Ryan ran over to join in the family hug as tears fell from all of our eyes. Like countless times in the past, my siblings and I were being yanked out of our horrible situation and placed in heaven on earth only for Denise to come back like a ghost in the night and snatch us up with the help of the courts. The same system that was supposed to protect us and help us put us right back into the clutches of the devil each time we escaped and there was nothing we could do about it. We just had to try to protect each other the best we could and up to that point we had done an okay job.

We were doing okay until that second when I realized that one of the most important pieces of the puzzle was nowhere to be found. As I glared at Denise with that zoned out, glazed over, brain-dead junky look in her eyes, I knew he wouldn't be though. If she was anywhere around, it was guaranteed that my little brother Sha would be gone. He still couldn't stand the sight of her or to hear her voice because all of his wounds were too fresh. Despite how well I, he, and our sister Terricka's lives had been living with the Robinson's, Sha never forgot all of the horrible things our mother did to him, to us. He never forgot and probably never would forgive her. I don't think any of us would forgive her for the hell she put us through.

"Where's Sha?" I asked Tania with tears flowing down my cheeks as she wiped my eyes with her thumbs before kissing me on the forehead.

"He's in the tree house. I haven't been able to get him to come out since he saw them pull up. I'm so sorry, Tisha. I love you so much and we will fight for you guys. As soon as Michael gets home, he's going to see what can be done. I called him at work and he's on his way now. We L." Tania said before being rudely interrupted by my mother clearing her throat and smacking her lips.

I envisioned myself running over to the island and drop kicking her wacky, cracky ass right off the stool she sat on as she taunted me, smirking while rolling her eyes at my foster mother. I glared at Denise with malice from across the room as she continued to smirk before looking at the Dollar Tree watch on her arm.

"Uhh, we have to be going, so go get the mu... Go get Shamel so that we can go, Shartisha. The police will be looking for Ms. Shaterricka too, be sure to tell her THAT when she comes back." My mother said to my foster mother as I felt her words vibrate through my body.

Although she was trying her best to be nice and speak in a non-threatening manner, I could still hear the violent undertones in her voice and see the insane rage surging through her body. I knew that as soon as we were out of eyes reach the maniac who gave birth to us would make us regret the day were we conceived. That was a truth that we could count on.

I turned back to look at my foster mother with tears still flowing from my eyes as Denise continued to bicker behind me. I looked into Tania's loving, scared eyes and I couldn't help but to wonder if I would ever see her again. I couldn't help but to cling to her one last time before totally pissing Denise off.

"That's a fucking nuff!" My mother yelled before catching herself, holding her mouth with her hands while looking at Mrs. Lee with wide eyes.

I froze in my tracks, holding my breath and anticipating a total shit storm as I heard Denise get up from the island behind me. Part of me cringed, anticipating the heavy blow she could throw. However, another part of me prayed she would let the real her shine through for a second. I would take one of her punches to the head or elbows to the ribs just to expose the real her. I hoped in that moment her pills would wear off and she would be the raging lunatic no one else ever seemed to see, but was the same monster we had to endure abuse from our entire lives. If there was such a thing as luck, then my hugging Tania again as my mother walked closer would have set her off and caused the reaction I was looking for.

In a perfect world that's what would have happened. In a world designed for anyone other than a child of my mother's it would have been possible. However, the Lewis children were never visited by luck. We were cursed children who lived by circumstance and once again the sins of our mother was the circumstance that would cause us unbearable pain. I could feel the hair on the back of my neck and arms stand up as my mother sucked her teeth and began her stellar speech.

"I'm sorry everyone, my emotions got the best of me for a moment. I love my children so much, I just go overboard sometimes. Please forgive me." My mother said looking at Mrs. Lee and then my foster mother.

I saw Mrs. Lee soften after looking into Denise's eyes and seeing exactly what she wanted her to see. It was easy to see that my mother had woven her magical, druggie web around the lady like everyone else. It was like Mrs. Lee had hit the pipe herself and suddenly lost her damn mind. Denise had her under her spell and she was gone like a crack head in the projects with a $100 bill in his pocket. I felt defeated as I realized my mother had totally fooled Mrs. Lee and managed to ruin my life once again.

Like a true heroin addicted, con artist my mother had played on the kindness of her victims and their motherly instincts. I had to swallow down the lump in my throat when I looked back at Tania and saw a bit of softness behind her sorrow.

It was hard to accept but not impossible to believe that Denise had fooled her too. That's what she did, tricked people. The only problem was she could only fool people who didn't know how evil, low down, and trifling her ass could be. She couldn't fool me though because I knew her and I knew that she never had a good intention in her life.

All my mother ever cared about was herself and her drugs, which were both the reasons why she needed us back. She needed us back to inflict her pain upon us and to finance her drug habits through the form of government assistance. That's it. We were nothing more than a violent release and quick hit in her mind and she had made that clear for as long as I could remember. I knew the real her. I knew that she was nothing but a sadist, psychopath who sold her daughters for drugs, dipped her son in scolding water, and beat, starved, and tortured each of us since we were old enough to walk and talk. I knew and hated her for who she was and I wished everyone else could see what I saw. However, as she sniffled and cleared her throat before continuing her speech, I knew that she was about to win again.

"I love my kids, all three of them and I am so very sorry for everything that has happened. I have illnesses that cause me to behave in a manner I wouldn't normally behave in. I'm not trying to make excuses I'm just stating that mental illness and drug abuse are real issues that can hurt a person and their family. I know because it hurt mine and now I just want to get my family back together again. I'm back on my meds, clean of drugs 40 days, I'm on my way to being the mother I once was. I just need my children to give me another chance. Forgive me Tisha...Please!" My mother said pretending to cry as I felt her hand coming close to my back.

The heat from her palm seared my back and I felt the pure evil within her soul almost jump from her body into mine as emotions began to take over me. I rocked on my heels and shook while holding back my tears and the rage burning inside before quickly dashing out of the room, avoiding Denise's touch. It felt like the world was crashing down around me as I ran out of the kitchen, down the hall, and out of the back patio door with tears falling from my eyes. I could still hear Denise's voice as I burst out on to the door and deeply inhaled the fresh air. I could hear her crying for her audience and gaining the sympathy she wanted as I slammed the door behind me.

Once I slammed the door, silencing Denise's conniving voice I stood there for a minute with my eyes closed and fists clenched, thinking about all of the pain in my life. It hurt to think of all we had overcome to only be thrust back into turmoil, but I knew that regardless of what hell lie ahead I had to be strong. I hummed our Salvation song in my mind and quickly found the strength to push all of my hurt, anger, and fearful emotions to the back of my mind and put on a brave face for my brother. I took several deep breaths, thinking about what I would say to Sha before making my way across the huge, plush lawn to the two-story tree house he was held up in. When I made it to the little blue step ladder leading up to the bright yellow, hatch door, I reached up to ring the bell but Sha opened the door before I could even touch the string.

"We have to go back, don't we, Tisha?" Sha asked, looking down at me with those sad, troubled eyes that were wise beyond their years.

I almost burst out into tears staring at the little brother I loved so much, but couldn't protect from the one person who was supposed to love him the most. I wished that at 10-years-old my brother didn't have to from suffer memories that would haunt him the rest of his life. I wished that I could take all of his pain away and give him the healthy, happy life he deserved. If wishes were dollars, I would have been a millionaire, but they weren't so all I could do was try to ease my brother's mind and my own at the same time.

I had to convince him and myself that everything would be okay when we left with Denise, even though my heart and mind were telling me something completely different. My heart told me to prepare for the disaster. My mind told me that I hadn't seen the worst of my mother yet. As I stood there staring up at my little brother with brave eyes and a crumbling heart, I knew that both my heart and mind were right. I knew that pain was in our near future if we left with Denise, but there was nothing I could do. She always found us no matter where we went, and when we were found we were always brought back. I couldn't fight that. I just had to do my best to make things bearable, like I always did.

I managed a big smile at Sha before motioning him down from the tree house as I gathered my thoughts.

"You know I can't be climbing trees with your niece or nephew in my stomach, boy. I have to be careful, no more jumping off roofs like Bat Girl." I said laughing as Sha stepped down on to the ground in front of me and smiled before touching my stomach.

For that brief second my brother looked so happy and peaceful as he touched my stomach, ignoring the world around him. He was so calm and serene I almost didn't want to interrupt his happiness with the ugly truth. However, I knew that I had to. I owed him the truth no matter what.

"Yes Sha, we have to go back." I said to Sha suddenly as he immediately stopped rubbing my stomach and attempted to go back into the treehouse.

I grabbed Sha's arm pulling him back into my arms as he cried and tried to break free.

"No Tisha, I won't go back. She is crazy and she does awful things to us. I hate her, she's a monster. Why can't anybody else see that? Why won't anybody help us? Why won't you help us, Tisha?" My little brother said while crying hysterically as I turned him around in my arms so that I could hug him head on.

Sha held me tight and allowed all of the tears that were penned up inside of him out as I rubbed his back and hummed the words to our Salvation Song in his ear. I could feel Sha's tight, tense shoulders and arms soften in my embrace as my love and the melody of the song soothed his aching heart. I knew what he was feeling, oh too well. And there was nothing more I wanted than to take away his fear and anxiety. However, I doubted I would ever be able to do that. What I could do was assure him that I would be right there with him until the end, no matter what, so that is what I did.

"Sha, I know it's scary to even think about going back, but we have to. We know the courts don't work for us and that lunatics like mama have more rights than anyone. I can't promise you that things will be different when we go back home with Denise this time, because I'm sure they won't be. What I can promise you though, is that I will be here for you. I will protect you Sha. I won't let her hurt you and when the first opportunity presents itself I'll get us out of there. Just roll with me in hell a little while longer lil brother. It's just me and you on the inside now and we'll have to get Terricka to work from the outside. If we stick together, we can get away from Denise for good. You just gotta trust me. Okay?" I asked Sha as a tear fell from my eye and he wiped it away.

I looked into my little brother's sad, tortured eyes and I saw a deep sorrow and an unwavering strength. Just like Terricka and I, Sha had lived through hell, survived, and developed a calculating, unrelenting strength that emanated through his eyes. I could see the fight still in him as he managed a weak smile before nodding his head at me.

"I trust you big sis, you know I do. I trust you and Terricka with my life and I know that if no one else cares, y'all do. I'm just scared, Tisha, but I'm gonna be strong and I'm gonna help protect you. I won't let her hurt you anymore or hurt the baby in your stomach. I love you, Tish."

Sha said as he hugged me tightly and I hugged him back as tears ran down my face.

I held my brother and cried one last time before drying my eyes, grabbing his hand, and bravely walking into the valley of the shadow of death.

Chapter 2

"The Lord is my Shepard; I shall not want.

He maketh me to lie down in green pastures:

He leadeth me beside the still waters.

He restoreth my soul:

He leadeth me in the paths of righteousness for His' name sake.

Yea, though I walk through the valley of the shadow of death,

I will fear no evil: For Thou art with me;

Thou rod and thy staff, they comfort me.

Thou preparest a table before me in the presence of mine enemies;

Thou annointest my head with oil: My cup runneth over.

Surely goodness and mercy shall follow me all the days of my life,

And I will dwell in the House of the Lord forever."

Echoed lightly from my lips as I leaned my head against the car window, watching the world pass me by while I was led to hell.

I recited that prayer along with our Salvation Song over and over again as Denise raged from the passenger seat and her new boyfriend snickered as he drove. I glanced over at Sha with tears in my eyes as he sat in the seat with his knees pulled up to his chest and his head tucked out of sight. I could see him shivering and his body flinch every time that Denise cursed from the front seat. I tried my best to drown her out as I turned back around and put my head back on the window; however it was too hard. I couldn't help but to listen to the venom that poured out of her mouth as I wished I was anywhere but in that car—even dead.

"Yea, but lil bitch I got yo funky ass now. Y'all hoes left my house like y'all was some muthafucking G's. Lil bitches sticking muthafuckas and robbing them in MY HOUSE ..MY FRIEND! I got something for your ass now though. I'ma get Terricka funky ass too, just watch I know where her and them lil pussies she call gang members hang. I'm going to get that lil bitch then both of y'all gonna pay ya fare ..like old times!" My mother said as I felt a sudden surge of nausea.

I couldn't believe she was suggesting that I sell my body for her drug habit again, knowing that I was pregnant. I would kill myself before I did something as stupid as that. Just the thought of doing something so foul made me dry heave as tears rolled down my cheeks.

"She can't hoe Denise, she pregnant. At least she can't sell pussy. But I bet you can find something else for her to do." My mother's new boyfriend, whom she called Duck said as he peered at me in the rearview mirror.

I rolled my eyes and mouthed the words, 'Fuck You' to him in the mirror as he snickered and flashed his crooked, gold smile. I couldn't stand him from the second I laid eyes on his high yellow ass with that nappy afro, those big pop eyes, freckles, and mouth full of gold teeth. He looked just like a dime store pimp who had lost all of his hoes in a card game, tired as fuck. I knew that he would only add to my trouble from that first second we met because as soon as he laid eyes on me he looked me up and down, undressing me with his eyes as he sucked his teeth. I knew right then that he was just like my mother and every other man I had met besides Jerrod, an inflictor of pain. He proved that as he laughed at me in the mirror before licking his tongue out, just as Denise exploded.

"YEAAAHHHHHHH, that's right. She did say the lil hoe pregnant, didn't she? Whose baby is it, Tisha? Do you even know bitch? I knew it would be you out fucking for free and getting caught up with a baby. Sensitive little naïve ass bitch, HOE YOU MAKE ME SICK!! I swear I should have swallowed or spit that night I conceived yo dumb ass. Worthless bitch! You and that fucking retarded mute all balled up back there, two NOTHING MUTHAFUCKAS. The robots told me long ago to get rid of you bitches and I didn't want to do it because the checks be coming right on time. But, now I'm like fuck it… I should. You ain't gone be shit anyway are you, Tisha? So what you finished high school early with the help of the foster bitch. ANNDDD, what you gonna do with it? Not a damn thang! You ain't gonna do shit but layup with lil niggas for free, like that Jerrod nigga. Oh, yeah you didn't think I knew about him did you?" My mama asked as I turned to look at her with tears all over my face as she smiled.

"Yea, I know about the lil bastard and I also know he in the gang with Terricka. I can't prove it, but I know he did something to Jerome too because he didn't just disappear. Y'all lil muthafuckas didn't get over on me. I'ma get him, but in the meantime tell me who the fuck yo baby daddy is SHARTISHA!" My mother yelled as she unbuckled her seatbelt and turned around in her seat facing me.

My heart raced like a herd of wild horses as I thought about how I should answer the question that the lunatic staring me down from the front seat was asking. I knew that honesty was supposed to set you free; however, with my mother's delusions were like sunsets; constant and they appeared at different times every day. In my mother's world, truth had no place and it was never welcomed. Telling my mother a truth she didn't want to hear was like spitting in her face, a violation which was punishable by severe pain. Just thinking about the ass kicking I'd get if I told my mother that the baby growing inside of me was in fact Jerrod's baby and we were getting married, made me shiver.

I looked up and met my mother's gaze as she stared at me with more hate, anger, and ill intentions I knew were possible. I couldn't even look at her long as her eyes penetrated my soul and made me feel a chill deep in my bones. I turned back to stare out of the window, laying my head against it again as tears fell from my eyes and my mind reeled. I wished at that moment that I could morph my brother and myself out of that car and to a parallel world where Denise didn't exist. I wished that my entire life was a dream, a long ass nightmare I had to see through until the end in order to get back to my real life. I wished and went over a dozen scenarios in my mind as I sat there with my head on the window, gazing out at the world as Denise huffed like a dragon behind me.

I knew that I didn't have long to ignore her before she would react though, so I tried to think of something to say that would satisfy the bipolar beast breathing like an obese dragon in the front seat. I closed my eyes, trying to think as I swallowed down the lump in my throat, hoping Denise would grow tired of waiting and move the fuck on. If I had any type of luck that would have happened. However, like countess times before, luck never visited the Lewis kids so it shouldn't have been surprised me when suddenly I felt a blow to the back of my head. The unexpected punch was so hard it made my head bounce off of the window and then slam back against it with so much force that my nose bust on impact.

Blood splattered all over the window, splashing back in my face as I cried out in pain before grabbing my nose. Denise was on me in a flash, grabbing me up in the back of my hair with one hand and choking me with the other as Sha screamed and clawed at her face. I tried to squirm out of her grip as she held me in my hair firmly, choking me tightly while whispering threats in my ear. However, no matter how much I struggled my weak, defeated, pregnant teenager strength was nothing compared to her possessed, bipolar, psychotic, and drugged out, lunatic strength. All I could do was try to reach out to push my brother back as I felt the air slowly leave my body and everything begin to go dim.

Sha screamed my name as I felt my body go limp in my seat. I peered through my blurred vision to see his worried, tear streaked face just before Denise released my throat, back-handing him so hard that he bounced off the door and slumped down to the floor. I gasped for air while trying to call Sha's name as what I saw began to sink in. Seeing my little brother hurt while trying to defend me ignited a rage in me similar to Denise's, a rage I never knew possible. In an instant that insane rage consumed me, causing sweet little Tisha to step out of character. Before my mother turned to wrap her hand back around my throat. I had jumped with the shit, turning the tables on her evil ass for the first time. It was like my body was moving on its own because the next thing I knew my thumbs were in her eyes as I pressed down as hard as I could, just like Jerrod had taught me.

I tried to dig the beast's eyes out of their sockets as she yelled out in agony and pure shock while punching me in the head with her free hand. Although, I was being punched in the head and jerked around mercilessly by my hair at that moment, I still felt a slight sense of victory for finally being able to give Denise some of the same pain she dished out right back. My victory was the shortest one in history though because before I knew it those blows to the head she was delivering with precision, had become too much. I blacked out in the backseat of the car as my mother continued to yank my hair and pound me in the head. The last things that I heard were the worried cries of Sha as he cowered on the floorboard and the shrill laughter of the lunatic's boyfriend as he taunted me from the driver's seat. After that all that was left was darkness and that same prayer echoing in my mind as I drifted; free of hurt and all pain.

The strong smell of alcohol and the low hum of a distressed air conditioner woke me up some time later. I opened my eyes and tried to focus on the things around me to figure out where I was, but the pain in my head and back was so excruciating all I could do was cry out for help. I closed my eyes and let my head fall back on the bed of nails I was on as my body began to shake and shiver from all I had been through. In less than 24 hours I had went through some of the most horrible events of my life, yet something inside of me was saying that I still hadn't seen the worst yet. I went from finding out where my loved lived, only to go there and find him missing. If that wasn't bad enough, I went back home to my happy world to find Denise there waiting for me. Like a black cloud or cancer out of remission, Denise was always right there when we were our happiest, ready to break us right back down.

Like always my life was nothing but a tragedy, a sad story in which I was forced to suffer the sins of my mother. The only difference this time was the fact that I had to face it all alone. I didn't have my sister right by my side like I always did. There was no Terricka to take some of the punches for me or to offer her shoulder to lean on. No, I was alone and forced to be Sha's protector as well as my own. The only problem was that in my condition I couldn't protect anyone. All that I could do was lay there on that raggedy metal cot and cry as flashes of my bleak life flashed before my eyes. I tried to imagine the silver lining in my situation like I used to do when I was younger but as I squinted my eyes to see through the darkness, realizing I was in a room not much bigger than closet, I knew that there was no pot of gold at the end of the rainbow. Hell, from the looks of the jail I was locked in I couldn't even imagine there being a rainbow. Like my life, there was nothing but rain, hail, and storm clouds everywhere.

I looked down, peering through the darkness to see that I was laying on a dirty, thin mattress that had exposed springs poking through it that were pressing into my back. The rusty metal pierced my skin, causing the excruciating pain I felt when I first opened my eyes. I tried again to lift my aching, battered body up off the cot I was on, but as soon as I lifted my head again everything began to spin. Sudden waves of nausea and shivers took over me as I cried out for help in the darkness, hoping someone would come to save me.

"Help me… Help ME. SOMEBODY….Please help me!" I cried as the door to the room I was in suddenly opened, letting in the bright light from the hall.

I used my arm to shield my eyes from the light as I tried to see who had come into the room. I didn't have to wonder who had entered long though because before I could open my mouth to ask who it was, the shrill, insane laughter of my mother off her meds filled the air, causing the hair on my arms to stand up.

"Ahhhhh, yea I'm back, Tisha. I'm back and I'm still with the shit. Now lil wanch are you gonna tell me what the fuck I wonna know? Who yo baby daddy, SHARTISHA? The robots said it's Jerome's or is it my boyfriend Chuck's? I know he was creeping with you or your hoeish sister. Bet you stupid bitches didn't get no money. You got something though, didn't you? WHO'S BABY IS IT, SHARTISHA?" My mother yelled from the doorway as I finally adjusted my eyes enough to see her.

I quickly wished I wasn't able to see my nasty, demented, crack whore of a mother as she stood in the doorway with a dingy pink lace panty and bra set on with a cigarette hanging from her mouth. She looked like a fucking sadistic clown with her hair matted to her head, big pink circles of rouge on her cheeks, with bright red lipstick smeared all over her lips while dangling a long, thick leather belt which was wrapped around her hand. She had the most deranged look I'd ever seen in her eyes as she deeply inhaled the cigarette and blew circles with the smoke as she walked towards the bed.

I flinched and tried to scoot back on the bed away from my mother as she laughed and continued to walk closer. However, the more I scooted, the more the raggedy, rusted metal dug into my back, ripping my flesh. I screamed out in agony as I flipped my body over on to my side, sliding my back up against the wall. I could feel the thick, warm blood as it poured from my wounds and trickled across my back, wrapping around my side as I watched my mother with wide, tear-filled eyes walk to the foot of the bed. I held my breath and prayed the imminent torture would be over quickly; however, I knew that I could never get off that easy. From the deranged look in my mother's eyes, I knew that my torture would be long, and hard, just like my life in her house.

I continued to hold my breath while staring intensely at the cigarette in Denise's hand as she puffed it long and hard, causing the fire on the end to become bright red and pointy. She held the cigarette between her thumb and index finger, rolling it from side-to-side as she smirked at me and sucked her teeth. All that I could do was lay there and watch her in terror as my heart beat in my throat and she began her new rampage.

"Lil bitch you just going to lay there like you don't hear me asking you a damn question. You acting like I won't beat yo ass into a coma again. ANSWER MY DAMN QUESTION SHARTISHA! You think you got welts all over yo ass now, don't answer me and I'll bust yo shit wide open. You hear me bitch?" Denise screamed at me like the psychopath she was as I trembled.

I tried to shake my head yes to let my mother know that I understood what she was saying, but every muscle inside of me felt stiff, almost catatonic as I laid there anticipating the worse. The worse is exactly what I got too, as Denise stuck the pointy, red hot fire from the cigarette into the bottom of my right foot. The searing pain from the fire shot through my body like electricity, causing me to scream out for mercy.

"PLEASE MAMA, PLEASE. I'LL TELL YOU...I'LL TELL YOU!" I screamed as Denise stuck the cigarette to the bottom of my left foot just for kicks as she began laughing.

I was able to pull my legs up to my stomach, wrapping my burned feet in the covers as Denise taunted me, still waiting on her answer.

"That shit hurt, didn't it lil bitch? Tell me then and this will all be over. Is it the Jerrod nigga's? If it is, he needs to pay what the fuck he weigh or I'm getting his ass locked up again. I know he grown as fuck so either he gonna pay me for y'all lil bastard child or he gonna go his pedophile ass to jail. It's y'all choice. Now tell me the truth, Shartisha!" My mother demanded as she rushed around to the side of the bed, pulling me to her by my hair as I screamed from the pain surging through my body.

I tried to think of the perfect person to frame and break my mother's fucking heart with as I punched at her and tried to unwrap her hands out of my hair. At that moment I was in an anger induced trance, consumed by my thoughts of revenge...vengeance. I was able to drown out my mother's curses and block her blows as I thought about who I could name that would hurt her the worse. I knew that there was no man my mother really cared about other than the dope man, and her secret married lover Renaldo, a retired Marine who smoked crack and fucked my mother whenever he was on leave and in the hood slumming. She was his project jump-off he used to escape the real world and live out his sick fantasies with. He would buy thousands of dollars' worth of drugs and alcohol whenever he was in town from Florida and him and my mother would have a wild, week-long party in which anything could happen.

Once, when I was 10 years old, I walked in on my mother fucking him from the back with a big, pink strap on dick as he moaned and squealed like a pig with a black leather mask over his face, and muzzle in his mouth. The whole sick ass scene looked like something straight off a sadistic flick and made me puke up all the noodles I had just eaten. That was one of the first times I realized my mother truly loved the vulgar, disrespectful man who gave her the money to support her habits while treating her like an animal. When he saw me staring at them that day with wide, scared eyes, he demanded she fuck him harder before telling her to call me into the room. I remember trying to run, but being caught by my mother as she jumped up to chase after me with the pink, glossy penis strapped to her waist bobbing in the air.

I screamed and clawed for my life as my mother drug me back into the room and threw me on the bed in front of him. I blocked out most of what happened that day, but what I do remember is he gave my mother an ultimatum to either watch him touch and fondle me or he would leave forever. Needless to say, that was a day I buried in the back of my mind with all of the other travesties. The only thing that's still fresh is the vision of my mother's face as she cried and begged

Renaldo to stay, telling him how much she loved him and would do whatever he asked. I had never seen my mother be a slave to anyone or anything other than drugs up until that point. However, after seeing her crawl for the half black, half Cuban prick she called Papi, I knew that he was her weakness. He would also be the perfect person I could use to get a little revenge.

I swallowed down the lump in my throat and tried to stop the butterflies from fluttering madly in my heart as I weighed out my options. After a few seconds of thinking as Denise continued to hold me in my hair and curse in my face, I blurted out the words that made my mother's heart stop and gave her a quick glimpse in the mirror. She froze in her tracks while still cursing as she stared at me, the enraged, carbon copy of herself.

"IT WAS YO NIGGA BITCH...RENALDO. RENALDO MY BABY DADDY, DENISE, AND HE SAID WE GETTING MARRIED AND HE GONNA BE A GREAT FATHER. HE LOVES ME YOU CRAZY, UGLY BITCH, NOT YOU. I WIN!!" I yelled to the top of my lungs, spewing the vicious words out of my mouth like venom.

The second those words left my mouth I knew that I had fucked up because my mother instantly released my hair and became silent. I looked up into her face as I scooted back to the wall and held my hands out in front of me. I expected the lunatic, who abused me all of my life, to jump on top of me like a spider monkey when she heard those words, but she didn't to my surprise. Instead of going in and beating me like the normal her would do, my mother simply turned around and left the room, locking the door behind her.

As soon as the door closed and I heard the lock turn, I finally released the breath I had been holding the entire time. Tears streamed down my face as I rubbed my belly and prayed that God would see me and my baby through. I wished that I could have Jerrod there with me; protecting me and telling me that everything would be okay. I needed him, I needed someone, anyone, but no one was there as I looked around my prison. I laid there for hours praying and crying, hoping that my pain would soon end. I laid there lost in my pain until I could see the sunset in the small window next to the door. As darkness crept up all around me and the bleakness of my situation began to set in, I opened my mouth and did the only thing I knew to do when I could do nothing else. I started to sing. I sang a song from my heart, all alone and helpless I sang a song of strength that I hoped would see me through.

"You may try to break me down,

But never count me out.

Despite all of the pain you cause,

I will never ever doubt.

The fact that I am blessed,

And my life deserves a chance.

So I'm stepping out on faith,

Putting my life in the Most High's hands.

I forgive you for it all,

But I will never ever forget.

All the things you put me through,

But still I live with no regrets.

What don't kill you makes you stronger,

I lived through hell and I'm still holding on.

So just listen to my message,

As I pour my heart out in this song.

All I want is endless hope,

And someone to help me please.

So I'm praying and I'm begging,

I'm down on bended knees.

When will my pain end?

Who can save a cursed soul?

Can you look into my eyes?

And see the pain and secrets that they hold.

Because I am..

I am Strength

I am.. Strong willed

I am Determined

With a faith you can't kill.

I am a cursed child but all of that can change,

So don't you count me out,

Just remember my name…

I AM STRENGTH!!!"

I sang from my heart as my tears soaked my pillow and I rocked myself to sleep. I drifted off with images of me and Jerrod happily ever after dancing in my head.

Chapter 3

I woke up to the rough tug of someone pulling on my arm as I quickly opened my eyes and looked directly into Denise's enraged face. I tried to call out to her and beg for her forgiveness, but there was something hard in my mouth, pressing down on my tongue and preventing me from speaking without some pain. Panic began to rise up from my stomach into my throat as I looked down to see that I had been stripped down to my panties and bra and that both of my legs and my left arm were already tied to the bed. Denise pressed down hard on the bend of my right arm like she was trying to snap it in half before she yanked it once again, popping my shoulder out of place.

My hysterical screams filled the air as Denise laughed and continued tying my arm to the bed post. The pain in my shoulder was so overwhelming I could barely catch my breath. I felt the muscles in my shoulder tear and rip as Denise tied the electrical cord around my wrist as tight as she could. My mother had such an intense, hateful look on her face as she secured me to the bed, I had to look away. I glanced over to the side to look at myself in the small, dirty mirror over the dresser on the opposite wall as the bed, and I saw that the hard thing in my mouth was some type of muzzle. I couldn't believe my eyes as I stared at my filthy, battered body tied up and muzzled like an animal, covered in blood, tears, and filled with fear. I was like a sitting duck; helpless and unable to defend myself against the beast who birthed me.

Tears rolled down the side of my face fast and hard as I looked back at my mother unraveling the extension cord in her hand as water dripped off of it on to the floor. I gasped when I saw the stream coming off the cord and droplets of water disappear into the carpet. I knew that I was staring at one of my mother's new ways to torture me and break me until I did her will. I knew that cord represented severe pain and I wouldn't be able to escape it. I could do nothing as I lay there with wide eyes tied to the bed with a muzzle in my mouth. I could do nothing but hope that my mother would have mercy enough not to kill my baby. I pleaded with her using my eyes for a second, and for a moment she showed something that resembled compassion, or the ability to be human. I couldn't believe it as she leaned over and pulled the muzzle out of my mouth so that I could speak.

"Please mama…Please Stop! I didn't mean it. This baby isn't Renaldo's, I promise. Please mama. I don't know whose it is. Just like you said I'm a stupid little hoe and I don't know who my baby daddy is. Please don't make my baby suffer for my sins though mama. Please!" I cried hysterically as my mother began to wind the extension cord around her hand, preparing to exact her revenge.

I could see nothing but malice and the need to make me feel pain in her eyes as she smirked at me and circled the bed, holding her arm with the extension cord in it high over her head. She flinched at me a few times like she was going to strike as she laughed and paced the floor, and every time she did it my heart raced and I felt like I would pass out. I could see satisfaction in my mother's eyes as she watched my tears soak the back of my hair and my body tremble from fear. She was feeding off of my trepidation, gaining more energy to be evil. I knew that I had to fight the panic inside of me and not show her my pain. I knew that was the only way it would end quickly, so I sucked up my tears. I held my breath as Denise put the muzzle back in my mouth while cursing me out. She screamed and raged for a few seconds, trying to build up fear in me before delivering the first of 40 lashes that she would give me.

"Don't kill yo baby, huh? Is it Renaldo's baby then bitch? Huh? Is it?" My mother screamed so loudly I felt my ears pop along with the searing pain from the extension cord cutting through the flesh on my thighs as she lashed me like a slave owner.

I swallowed down my screams, biting down on the muzzle, and blowing out my breath as Denise sliced me again in the same spot. I was in real mental warfare as I fought the natural instincts inside of me to yell and scream. I was able to fight it though as tears rolled down my cheeks but no sounds came from my mouth. The only noise I made was when I firmly answered Denise's question while biting the muzzle. I gave her none of the satisfaction she gained from my pain and fear as I stared at that evil bitch without whimpering or showing any signs of giving in.

"No, don't kill my fucking baby and hell no this is not Renaldo's baby." I yelled to my mother in a distorted voice, biting down on the muzzle between words as she put her face so close to mine I could see up her nostrils.

I tried to control the rage building inside of me as I stared my tormentor in her eyes, and she snarled like a demented beast. My mother hissed and spit in my face through clenched teeth as I held my breath and fought the rage steadily building inside of me.

"Naw bitch, I ain't gonna kill yo baby. Duck and the robots convinced me that letting you keep the baby is best. That baby equals another check in my eyes so it WILL stay alive. However, you are gonna do what I say. If I bring a muthafucka in here for a hand job or to get his dick sucked, yo ass is gonna do it. I don't wonna hear shit about it either, Tisha. You buck bitch and Sha will get his ass beat right now. Do you understand me? You owe me, Tisha. I don't know if I believe you about Renaldo or not, but I'm gonna continue to beat that ass until I feel better." My mother said as she continued to strike me all over my arms, legs, chest, and shoulders with the wet extension cord.

A few of the slices from the extension cord my mother was swinging wildly like a psychopath hit me across the stomach, causing me to yelp out in pain despite my stern resolve to remain silent. I couldn't fight that natural reaction to show pain and try to defend myself as I tugged against the cords while crying, trying to break free. My mother continued to laugh in her eerie, deranged cackle as she leaned back in close to my face and laughed at my pain. Tears flooded my eyes clouding my vision as I stared at the distorted face of the person I hated the most. She taunted me with her words, stirring up my vexation to the point where I was about to explode.

"Hurts don't it wanch? That's what you get you little rotten bitch. You know what, Tisha? I wish you were never born. I couldn't stand your bitch ass father and you turned out to be a big piece of nothing just like him. All of you muthafuckas have. I gave up everything to have you bitches and y'all have brought me nothing but grief. That's okay though. You about to pay me back for the money I lost while y'all was kicking it with the fucking Brady Bunch. Yeah bitch, you gonna pay me back or I'm gonna beat that little mute next door until he has no choice but to scream and let me hear his voice." My mother threatened me, still so lose to my face that the spit flying from her mouth landed in my eye.

I shook and growled like a pit bull while biting down on the muzzle and staring into my mother's glossy eyes. Her words made the hate in me push forward breaking through the fortress I had around my emotions. Tears streamed down my face as the words she spat out of her mouth like poison penetrated my heart.

"Now what you gonna do, Tisha? The quicker you realize I run this shit and you WILL do what I say the better off you will be. When yo funky ass turn 18 you can go, but Sha and possibly the baby will stay with me. If it's a girl maybe I can get some good work out of her too." My mother said laughing as I took all of the anger and pain I had inside and used it to head butt her sick ass right in the face.

The impact of my hard ass head hitting my mother square in her nose caused it to bust on impact. Blood splattered everywhere as my mother yelled out in pain and I broke out into hysterical laughter. I cursed my mother and told her how much I hated her through my muffled, muzzled voice while watching her as she held her bloody face in her hands. I felt victorious for a second as my mother cowered over to the side of the bed and I continued to laugh at her pain. It felt good to fight back. It felt damn good to finally stand up for myself and not be my mama's personal victim anymore. I was tired of it, and even if it meant she would beat me and my baby to death right then, at least we wouldn't have to be with her. I was willing to be anywhere other than where I was at that moment.

After what seemed to be five minutes, my mother suddenly popped up into a standing position like a possessed jack in the box. I flinched when she turned around quickly and rushed into me swinging the extension cord again and hitting me wherever it landed. For about four minutes straight my mother beat me mercilessly everywhere that she could as I cried and gasped for air. I blacked out several times throughout the entire ordeal and every time that I opened my eyes I was met by either a slice from the extension cord or a slap to the face. One time I woke up to the a sharp sting in my right leg followed by a deep, bone scraping pain as Denise began rubbing salt into the wounds on my legs she left behind. The pain was so overwhelming I blacked out again as my mother whispered in my ear how much she hated me.

I woke up several times after that as she continued to curse me out before sitting beside me on the bed smoking meth from a big, cloudy glass pipe. The smoke she blew out was thick, white, and stifling as I gasped for air through my pain. I cried for my mother to help me and asked about Sha several times when I woke up, but each time she either laughed or continued to get high while sitting next to my bleeding, battered body like I wasn't even there. She burned me on my legs and arms with her meth pipe a few times before I let the exhaustion and pure delirium the pain brought, suck me into a coma-like sleep. I welcomed the relief that the darkness brought, only then could I escape the pain. I dreamed about Jerrod and I living happily ever after with our baby far away from Denise as my blood stained the sheets and thin mattress I laid on.

The sound of someone breathing heavily and the feeling of being watched were the first things I noticed when I opened my eyes the next morning. It was April the third and I had been locked in the dungeon my mother prepared for me for two whole days with no water or food, and nowhere to relieve myself. The smell of urine was strong in the room as I had been forced to pee on myself or hold it and harm my baby. Lack of food had made it easy for me to hold my bowels up until then, but as I stared at the sick face of my mother's rapist boyfriend, Duck, I wondered would it continue to be easy. I felt my stomach do flips as I glanced through the fog and saw him sitting on the bed next to me rubbing himself. At that moment I suddenly felt like I couldn't hold my bowels anymore.

I looked down and noticed that my mother had removed the muzzle from my mouth while I was unconscious so I quickly parted my lips and prepared to scream for my life as the creepy fucker sitting next to me began to trace my inner thigh with his fingertips. I tried my hardest to scream but no matter how much I strained and pushed, barely any sound came out of my mouth. My throat was so dry and I had cried so much for so long, nothing would come out no matter how hard I tried. Crocodile tears ran down the side of my head as I begged Duck to leave me alone and he laughed while continuing to move his hand farther up my leg.

"Please leave me alone. I'm pregnant. Please don't touch me and disrespect my baby." I begged as my head began to spin and everything became blurry.

It was like everything was a dream or I had suddenly gotten extremely high as I looked up at the creep with blurry vision as he smiled that sneaky, crooked gold smile and leaned in to whisper in my ear while untying my right hand. My arm hit the bed hard due to my dislocated shoulder and I screamed out in agony, drowning out Duck's words as I screamed for him to help me before blacking out again. When I came to Duck had popped my shoulder back into place and had my hand on his dick as he moaned and rubbed my titty while whispering in my ear.

"See princess I can help you if you let me. I can make it all stop believe me. If you are nice to me, I'll be nice to you. All you gotta do is play ball. I just need you to play with my asshole a little and lick my chest. That's it. That's not much to ask a person who will save you a lot of pain. Is it?" The fucking pervert in front of me asked as he stuck his slimy, wet tongue into my ear.

Nausea crept up on me fast and hard as I suddenly turned directly into Duck's face and puked out the only food I had in my stomach, which I had eaten two days before. Vomit spewed all over that bastard as he jumped up and began pacing in a circle while cursing. I just knew that he was going to beat me too and that I would lose my baby for sure after I saw him tremble while wiping vomit out of his eyes. However, when he suddenly started laughing I knew that he was a special kind of crazy I would regret ever laying eyes on. I trembled in a level of fear not even my mother could produce in me as I watched Duck turn around to face me. He had a deranged look in his eyes as he wiped a chunk of throw up off his face and licked it off of his finger. I threw up again after seeing him do some disgusting shit like that and I prayed that everything that was happening was a dream.

The room began to spin again as Duck walked back over to me and straddled my body. I could feel his breath on my neck as my vision began to get blurry and dimmer. The last thing that I felt was the weight of Duck's body on top of mine and his tongue on my neck followed by the sound of his heavy breathing in my ear. After that I was gone again, enveloped in darkness, free from my torture.

"Get yo ass up, Tisha!" My mother yelled, startling me out of my pain-induced coma some time later that afternoon.

Pain surged up and down my body as I opened my eyes and looked at my mother in her purple tights and purple and white Polo shirt. She appeared to be semi-sober and possibly on her meds, or at least a milder drug at the moment because her voice was so calm and rationale. I squinted my eyes and hid them from the light Denise flicked on as she walked over to the cot to release my left arm and legs. She paid no attention to the fact that one of my right arm was already untied, but I did as I remembered the flashes I had between black outs. I wondered was I dreaming or was it true that Duck had come into the room to mess with me when I was unconscious. I knew that my suspicions were true when my mother finally untied both of my legs, placing them on the floor while pulling me into a sitting positon and my bra fell off.

That was proof to me that Duck was indeed in the room and had offered me protection in return for sexual favors. It should have been clear to my mother too if she cared or was a sane person, but she wasn't so she simply fastened my bra back up while whispering in my ear.

"Now don't think because I'm gonna let you get up, clean you up, and give you some food I'm going soft or some shit. I still can't stand yo funky ass but I know we got some meetings coming up soon and I need you to look yo best. Don't get it twisted though bitch, you still owe me and you will pay…one way or another, Tisha. Now, you can go out here, take shower, and I'll tend to yo wounds so they won't get infected. After that you can clean up and then find you something to eat. I'm going out for a while. When I get back, I want you and Sha out of fucking sight and this house clean. Do you understand?" My mother asked me as she stood back to look me in the eyes so that I would know she was serious.

I bit my bottom lip and shook my head up and down, fighting back my anger and tears as I made sure my mother knew that I understood her.

"Now, I have the robots watching you so don't think you slick and try to runaway like you and yo funky ass sister good for. It's no use running because I'll always find y'all. I'm gonna get her bald headed ass too just watch and see and she will get it worse than you. Now be the little pussy, Tisha, you have always been and do what the fuck I say or else." My mother demanded as she yanked me up off the bed by my hands.

The pain in my stomach and legs was unbearable as I wobbled forward. I had to grab on to the raggedy furniture in the room in order to make it to the door safely as my mother's evil ass pushed me along from the back.

"Hurry the fuck up, Tisha. I don't have all day." My mother yelled from behind me as I tried to walk faster, but the pain in my stomach caused me to slump over and shuffle my feet when I walked.

When I made it to the door of the room, I was held in my mother swung it open revealing the hallway and I almost died from the pure filth before me. The crème colored walls of the hallway were stained with fingerprints, burn marks, and dirt and there was piles of trash, cigarette butts, and drug wrappers everywhere. Although Denise had moved out of the run-down apartment in Breezy Point we grew up in while we were in foster care, she had done no better moving into the filthy almost condemned, 3-bedroom, rat infested hell hole she was now in. I saw cracks in the ceilings, mold on the walls, and roaches crawling everywhere as I shuffled my sore, pregnant body down the hall passed the piles of trash stacked to the celling.

"This door right here." Denise yelled at me as we approached a door at the end of the hall on the left.

When my mother opened the door, the foul stench of human fecal matter hit my nose with such fury I thought I would pass out. I had to turn around and suck in some fresh air before allowing her to push me forward into the filthy bathroom. The white tile floor was black in the cracks and had hair, trash, and dirt all over it. The ring in the bath tub was so black, and thick I thought to myself how no amount of bleach and hard work could ever get it out. I felt my stomach churn as I continued to scan the filthy space and Denise stood behind me sucking her teeth.

"Uhh hmmm, uppity now, huh? What it's too nasty in here for you, Princess Tisha? Well, too bad bitch. If you don't like it do something about it. As a matter of fact that's what you gonna do. Since you think you can refuse paying me back, you will pay me back in work until I know you're ready. And YOU WILL BE READY. Now, take those fucking clothes off and get in the shower." Denise yelled, pushing me up against the tub.

I quickly peeled my bra and panties off as tears rolled down my face and I stepped into the tub. I felt like puking or better yet dying when my feet touched the soggy, slimy, bacteria filled bath mat inside of the tub. I stood there trembling rubbing the welts on my slightly protruding belly as Denise cut the hot water in the shower on in full force. I could tell from the smirk on her face that she expected me to scream out in pain, but I welcomed the soothing feel the hot water had on my wounds as I closed my eyes and embodied the relief. Denise spoiled my serene moment by slapping me across the face with a hand towel before handing me some Dial antibacterial soap. I took the items from her before rolling my eyes as she laughed and stepped back.

"You really think you scare me when you look like that don't you, Tisha? Well, you don't bitch. Don't NOBODY put fear in me, especially not a pussy like you. Now, wash them wounds so I can spray this shit on them to help them heal and then get the fuck out of here. Remember what I said though bitch. The robots watching you for me." My mother said as she twitched and then looked around at the corners of the bathroom ceiling like she really had cameras.

I shook my head in disgust as I washed myself the best that I could and then rinsed off. When I stepped out of the tub, I watched as my mother's eyes washed over my body and she sucked her teeth and rolled her eyes. I saw a hint of jealousy as my mother looked at my young, firm body, which was a body she once had but would never get again with all of the poison she pumped into herself. No, my mother's beautiful days were long gone and that was part of the reason she hated and resented me and my sister Terricka so much. We were everything beautiful and loving she could never be again.

A smirk spread across my face as I thought about my mother being jealous of me and she sprayed the wounds all over my body with an antibacterial, pain spray. The smell of the medicine was strong and overpowering; however, it offered instant relief from the deep cuts and welts on my skin, soothing the burning sensation and cutting the stench in the room.

"Put this on and hurry the fuck up." My mother yelled as she handed me a long, black, cotton gown with the words *Free Yourself* written across the front. I thought that was ironic as I pulled the gown over my head and pulled it down, wiping away my tears with the musky, stiff fabric.

"Okay let's go." My mother said as she grabbed my arm and escorted me out of the bathroom, back down the hall, and into the living room.

I stopped in the doorway as soon as I saw Duck sitting on the couch in the corner, surrounded by mountains of trash and clothes. The living room in this new apartment was even filthier than that one in our old apartment, which was something I never thought was possible. I rolled my eyes at Duck as I scanned the room looking at all of the beer bottles and cans, condom wrappers, Newport packs, and pizza boxes all over the floor. I couldn't believe that the courts had approved somewhere so fucked up for us to live, but obviously they had because we're there. Once again we were in hell with Satan's daughter and we had to deal with it. I watched Denise as she slipped on some dirty flip flops that were by the door and prepared to leave before turning to me again.

"Remember what I said, Tisha. They watching." My mother said as she opened the door to leave and Duck started laughing.

I looked at him and rolled my eyes again before turning to my mother and calling her name.

"Denise. Where is Sha? Let me see him PLEASE." I begged my mother as she froze halfway out the door with her back turned.

For a second I thought she was going to at least answer me, but when her laugh began to echo in the air I knew that wasn't going to happen. My mother walked out of the house and slammed the door behind her, leaving me standing there looking stupid with a sick pedophile cackling like a hyena behind me. Before I knew it tears began to stream down my face as my body shook uncontrollably. I couldn't control my emotions as I thought about the horrible things my mother may have done to my brother. I couldn't understand why she just wouldn't let me see him if he was okay, so I assumed that meant he was hurt bad or maybe worse, he was dead. I sobbed and wobbled on my feet as I turned back to Duck and pleaded with him to tell me where my brother was.

"Please, I know you hate me too, but please tell me where my brother is. Let me see him." I begged Duck as I slowly watched a glimmer of compassion build in his eyes.

I continued to cry and beg through slurred speech as I watched him put his Newport out and get up from the couch to come over to me. Part of me expected him to hit me or to do something perverse when he made it to me; however, he didn't. When Duck made it over to me, he simply wrapped his arms around me and pulled me into an embrace. Despite the evil I could see inside of him too, that single act of kindness showed me that he was at least a little better than my mother. At least he could show some compassion. I allowed Duck to keep his arm around my shoulder as he led me back down the hall right passed the room I was in to the closet next door. I felt my heart fall into my feet when he stopped me in front of the door, unlocking it and swinging it open revealing a small, very dark room.

I glanced at the inside of the open door when it was completely ajar and I noticed small scratch marks and blood towards the bottom before stepping forward inside. I called out Sha's name in the darkness of the closet and waited for him to say something back. After a second or two and no response, I stepped further inside as Duck hit the light switch in the hall illuminating the darkness inside. When I was able to adjust my eyes to the bright light in the closet and look down into the far right corner, I was totally shocked and taken aback by what I saw. What I saw inside of that closet was a horrific sight I would probably never forget. It was a sight that would help solidify the hate I felt

for my mother and give me the strength to slay that
dragon once and for all.

Chapter 4

Sorrow, regret, and guilt hit me all at once as I fell to my knees beside my battered and bloody brother, pulling his limp body up into my lap. Tears fell from my eyes and I cried my heart out as my brother, Sha coughed and moaned in my arms. I could barely stop my tears from flowing or hardly stand to even look at my brother's bruised, bloody, and swollen face as he moaned my name. I tried to suck up my tears and hide the terrified look on my face as Sha peered up at me through sad, swollen eyes, but my heart ached for the pain I knew he was in. All I could do was cry and tell him how much I loved him and that things would be okay.

I noticed that welts, cuts, bruises, and burns were all over my brother from head to toe as I sucked up my sadness and inspected his body. It appeared that after I passed out from the beating I received, Denise went to take her anger out on Sha. She beat him with the same extension cord that had cut through my skin and caused me excruciating pain. I couldn't believe the amount of hate and inhumanity my mother was capable of as

I glared at the burn in the shape of a cross on Sha's right foot while he shook in my arms.

"Tisha, it hurts. I didn't do nothing. She just came in the living room and grabbed me. I hate her, I hate her so much. I heard you screaming too. I tried to get out but I couldn't. I couldn't get out the door to help you, Tisha." Sha cried hysterically as I pulled him close in my arms and kissed his head.

My tears fell fast and hard as they ran down my face, on to my brother's forehead, and mingled with his.

"Shhhh Sha. It's gonna be okay. I love you little brother and I will protect you." I said through my tears as I stroked his cheek with my hand and prayed that God would hear our cries.

I cried and rocked back and forth holding my brother for a few minutes as I hummed the words to our salvation song and he clung on to me for dear life. During that time I thought about all of the pain my mother had put us through and how something better had to be around the corner. Although I had already been through some of the worse things imaginable, deep down inside I still believed that trouble didn't last forever. Somewhere inside of me beneath the anguish and turmoil was the old naïve, Tisha who believed in happy endings. She had to be there, she was the light. I needed the light to balance the darkness because without it I would drown.

"Come on Sha. I got you." I said to my brother after crying all I could cry, drying my tears, and gathering the courage to move on like I always did.

I picked Sha's frail, battered, 80 pound body up off the floor and carried him out of the coffin he was left to die in, despite the pain in my stomach, back, and head. I carried my brother to the room I was in and laid him on the bed before hurrying off to the bathroom. Once inside I rambled through the filth on the floor and counter until I found some of the items I needed to clean Sha's wounds and reduce his pain. I washed out and filled an empty ice cream container with water before grabbing the first aid items I found, and scurrying back to the room.

When I got back inside the room, Sha laid on the bed still and quiet like he was trying to melt into the mattress. For a second I thought he was dead as I inched closer with the bowl in my hand, dripping water on the floor while my heart beat in my throat. I gasped and then exhaled in relief when I got close enough to touch Sha and he suddenly turned his head looking at me. I smiled through the anxiety, fear, and sadness I felt inside as I sat the water down on the floor and began working on the wounds on my brother's back and legs.

Both Sha and I remained quiet as I cleaned the cuts and welts on his cocoa skin with alcohol and put Neosporin on them. Not a sound could be heard in the room until suddenly someone behind us smacked their lips and the smell of cigarette smoke filled the already musky air. I turned my head slightly to the left and looked out of the corner of my eye to see Duck standing there sucking on a Newport, looking like a fish while dangling a beer in the other hand. I rolled my eyes at him before turning back to my brother and continuing to work on his wounds.

"Don't be so evil, Ms. Tisha. Remember, Duck is your friend. You help me and I'll help you princess. I know y'all in hella pain. I can give you something that will help ease that pain, even safely in your condition. Hell, I can make it stop all together. All you gotta do is be nice. Remember that." Duck said as he laughed before puckering an air kiss to me while winking his eye.

I glared in his direction with so much hate I think it kind of scared him because he quickly stepped back with his hands in the air like he was surrendering. I watched him through hateful eyes as he turned to walk down the hall with that creepy ass laugh trailing behind him. Once he was out of sight and I could no longer hear the laugh that made my stomach quiver echoing in my ears, I went back to tending to Sha.

I tried to be as gentle as I could while dressing Sha's wounds, but it seemed that no matter how softly I touched him it hurt. He moaned and grunted the entire time I worked on him, but he didn't cry. I think he had cried out all of his tears and all that he had left was the grunts and moans that were coming out of his mouth. Just knowing that my baby brother was internalizing so much pain was devastating to me. However, despite the anguish churning inside as I put burn ointment on the walnut shaped burn near my brother's groin, I pushed through it. Crying internal tears while maintaining a brave face on the outside, I dressed all of Sha's wounds and made him comfortable in the concrete-like bed.

"I'll be back in a few minutes Sha. You just lay here and rest, okay?" Everything is going to be okay, I promise. I will protect you. I'm going to get food for you and I'll be back." I said to Sha as he grabbed my arm.

He looked at me with sorrow and pain emanating from his soul as I looked back with mirrored eyes. I hated that we shared a bond built on anguish; however, it was a bond so deep nothing or no one could break it. I loved my brother more than I loved myself and I was willing to give myself to keep him safe. I was willing to take all of the pain Denise had to give and anything Duck's sick ass could think up if that meant Sha was safe and I didn't have to be a human semen receptacle like my mama wanted. I would do whatever it took to protect the ones I loved, I just wished more people felt that way about me.

I kissed Sha's hand before releasing my shirt from his grip as he laid there with a pained look in his eyes staring at me. I could tell there was something on his mind that he really wanted to say and I was prepared to listen to him, or at least I thought I was. However, I wasn't ready for what came next. What Sha said next cut down to my soul and made it even more imperative in my mind that I get him out of Denise's house.

"Tisha, do you think there's really a heaven? And if there is a heaven and a God up there will he let me in when I die? I ask you that because I don't think God hears our prayers. He can't T, because I ask for help every day and every day mama is still there to hurt us. If there is a God, being with him would be the best place to be, wouldn't it? Well, that's where I wonna go then Tish. I just wonna die and go someplace no one can hurt me. I know mama won't be in heaven so that's where I wonna go." Sha said to me as I watched the pain in his eyes grow.

I rushed back over to my brother's side and grabbed his hand in mine as I laid my head on his chest and cried for the innocent, little boy he once was. It broke my heart to hear my 10 year old brother contemplate death and want to be anywhere our mother wasn't, even if that was dead. I knew that feeling though, which is why I could do nothing but cry as Sha wrapped his bruised and battered arms around my shoulders and comforted me. For a second he was the protector, and in that moment, in his arms I felt safe.

"Sha, there is a God, but you won't see him anytime soon. We just gotta be strong, we'll get through this like we always do. Now, please rest Sha. I'll get you something for the pain, just try to sleep." I said as my tears ran down my brother's chest and I attempted to get my shit together.

I rubbed my eyes with the back of my hands, grinding out my tears and sadness as I thought about what I had to do. I knew that I had to endure whatever was thrown my way until it was time to go. I knew that moving hastily could cost me dearly in the end so I had to plan our escape just right. In the meantime, I would do most of what I was told and try to keep Sha the fuck away from my mother's crazy ass as much as possible. I was way more concerned with his safety than my own and for the first time I saw that deep fear in his eyes too. The concern and fear I saw in Sha's eyes as I released his embrace and held my shoulders up high, was somehow different than any fear and hate that burned there before. I channeled my strength, pulling myself together as Sha looked at me with an eerie, almost serene expression on his face. It was like he knew something I didn't, like he knew change was coming.

"I'll be right back, Sha, just rest please." I said to my brother as I walked out of the room.

I could feel Sha's eyes on me as I walked into the hall way. When I got outside, I looked back inside to see him still laying there with that peaceful, serene look on his face. I should have felt comforted knowing that my brother had found some type of peace. However, the chill running through my body causing goosebumps to pop up all over my arms, told me I shouldn't rejoice just yet. That eerie feeling told me something was coming, but I couldn't see or stop the future. All that I could do was wait out the storm that was coming, and I was sure it was coming.

I made my way into the kitchen passed Duck who was back on the couch amongst mountains of trash, chain smoking Newports and guzzling his fifth beer. When I stepped into the disaster area that was supposed to be a kitchen, I almost vomited from the filth and horrific smells. Old food containers, dishes, boxes, trash, clothes, dirt, rats, roaches, paper, and baggies covered the floor and cabinets everywhere. There was not a spot in the disgusting ass kitchen that wasn't filthy or covered in some shit. I had to put my hand over my mouth to keep the vomit that was creeping up my throat down in my stomach. My eyes watered as I continued to hold my breath while walking deeper into the kitchen. The thought of tackling such a huge job on my own made me exhausted as I exhaled deeply while kicking a pile of newspapers near the sink and an army of roaches ran from underneath. My flesh crawled and I squealed in disgust as I ran forward like a lunatic, stomping and cursing roaches.

"This shit is gonna take me forever." I said to myself as I went over to the pantry and got out the broom, mop, and cleaning supplies.

It was apparent that no one had cleaned that kitchen in a very long time, if at all because the gallon sized bottle of Pine-Sol I found in the closet was still full and it had cobwebs hanging off of it. I had to rinse the cobwebs and thick layer of dirt off of the bottle before I could start cleaning. As I walked over to the sink which was filled with trash and crusty dishes, I felt as if someone was watching me. I could feel eyes on the back of my neck as I found a space to squeeze the bucket into the sink and let the brown, rusty water fill it. I knew that it was Duck watching me, lusting after me, but I wasn't about to even acknowledge his perverted ass.

I didn't even turn around, I just filled the bucket and began cleaning the sink and kitchen cabinets. As I cleaned I let all of my emotions rush forward, and fuel my body like coal to a locomotive. I moved about the disgusting room, robotically and methodically cleaning and releasing tears filled with anger and sadness. I could see Sha's battered face in my mind as I threw piles of trash out of the open kitchen window, getting my first glimpse of where I was being held. I quickly looked around with my upper body out of the window, noticing that I was in some apartments that had three stories to them.

I made a mental note of the color of the bricks, the houses on the street behind the apartments, and how high the perimeter fence was so that I would know exactly how Sha and I would have to escape. I couldn't jump off of any roofs like I had done in the past so I knew that I had to plan a ground route that would have less complications, for my baby's sake. I got lost in my daydream, inhaling the fresh air as my body still dangled out of the window. I got so lost I didn't even hear Duck behind me until he had his slimy hands on my waist, pulling me back inside of the window.

"Woooo there, Tisha. I can't let you kill yourself on my watch. How would that look?" Duck said laughing as I quickly stood up straight with my back to him and my face pressed up against the open window.

I could feel Duck's hot, cigarette, beer, and booty smelling ass breath on the side of my neck, creeping around to my face as he pressed his body up against mine before licking the back of my ear. My stomach churned and I had to hold my mouth to keep the vomit and screams threatening to break free down.

"Now Tisha, I know you weren't trying to get out were you? You up three floors little girl. In your condition, I wouldn't go jumping out of windows and shit like a super hero. Besides, wherever you go she'll find you. Yo mama crazy as shit and when she sets her mind on something she gets it done. I ain't never met a bitch crazier than her. I would have been quit fucking with her if it wasn't for the fact that she a complete freak and she got some fye ass head and good enough pussy. That's neither here nor there though. What a nigga saying is with a mammy crazy as Denise, you need allies. Let me be your ally, Tisha. You help me and I'll help you. I can make it all stop." Duck said as he reached around me and grabbed me tightly around the waist, pressing his penis into my butt as he moved his pelvis in a grinding motion.

I felt disgust, anger, and fear surge through me as I squirmed to get out of Duck's grip while elbowing and pushing him back.

"Get off of me. I have a man who I love. I don't want to help you, but as a human you should help me just because, knowing what my mother is doing. I shouldn't have to DO anything for you to help me. If you know she's crazy why would you let her continue to do this while you sit idly by? That's because you ain't shit either. Get the fuck out of my face!" I yelled to Duck as his face changed from a perverse look to one of astonishment, and then amusement.

Duck's cold, creepy ass laugh filled the air as he backed away out of the kitchen with his arms held up in the air. I watched him from the corner of my eye, not turning towards him and giving him the satisfaction of knowing I was afraid, I was though. As I stood there my heart raced and my legs wobbled so much I thought I would fall out of the open window. I calmed my breathing and finally stopped my legs from wobbling when I heard him get right outside of the kitchen door and stop. I held my breath and waited, watching my breath fog up the window my face was pressed against as Duck's laugh trailed off.

"Just know that the offer is available whenever you're ready pretty girl. Know that I will be waiting." Duck said sucking his teeth before disappearing down the hall.

He was so fucking creepy and disgusting he gave me the shivers, causing the hair to stand up all over my body as I tried to shake it off and get back to work. When I knew that Duck was completely gone, I was finally able to relax as much as possible in that situation. Over the three hours following that I worked diligently cleaning the kitchen, living room, bathroom, and even the room Sha was in as he laid there sleeping. I cleaned and cried with visions of my past and the love I longed for playing in my mind. I needed to see Jerrod and have his arms around me at a time when I wasn't sure if I would live or die. I wasn't even sure if I cared whether I lived or died at that moment as I thought about the miserable existence I had.

The only thing that gave me a second of hope was thinking about the few people who truly did love me; my boyfriend, my sister, and my brother. I thought about them and I knew that I had to be strong because they each faced their own version of hell and I was all they had. I cried for Jerrod being gone, I cried for my sister being lost, and I cried for my brother being broken beyond repair. I cried as I drug my exhausted body across the room finishing up the one-woman extreme home makeover I had just pulled off. I looked around at the clean, fresh kitchen in which you could now actually see the floor and cabinets, and I felt a twinge of pride beneath the extreme pain and hunger raging in me. I stood there huffing like an out of breath whale as the rumble from my stomach roared so loudly that's all I could hear.

"You did a damn good job, Tisha, damn good. Now come get something to eat." Duck said as he stood in the kitchen door with a crooked ass smile on his face.

I didn't know whether or not I should trust him as he stood there cheesing at me like a sneaky ass cat, but the aroma coming from the living room had me captivated. Apprehensively, I walked forward into the living room as Duck laughed and trailed behind me. Once inside I felt my stomach do flips as the KFC chicken, biscuits, mashed potatoes, gravy, and mac-n-cheese invaded my nostrils. I went straight to the table, making my brother and myself a plate loaded to the top with food before quickly scurrying off to the room. Once inside I woke Sha up and helped him to get a little food down before he moaned himself back to sleep.

I hated to see him in so much pain knowing that I could do something to help him. However, no matter what lie I told myself, I just couldn't bring myself to letting someone other than Jerrod touch me, not if I had any control in the situation. I sat there with tears rolling down my face as I stuffed food into my mouth and watched my brother moan and fight in his sleep. The internal fight he was having at that moment with the demon who haunted us was just like the one I was having with myself on whether I should give in to Duck. I cried until my throat felt sore and my body shook in violent hiccups.

I cried until my body slowly gave out on me and I fell asleep at the foot of the bed with my head on my brother's legs and the plate still in my hand. I woke up some time later to the sound of music blasting from the living room along with the sounds of people laughing. I quickly got up, sat my plate on the dresser, and tip toed over to the door, peering out to see that Duck had company and was having a party. I knew that if he partied anything like my mother did, trouble was around the corner so I quickly closed and locked the door before returning to the bed with Sha.

I smiled at my brother when I got back to the bed and noticed he was awake as he looked at me through glossy, serene eyes. He and I sat there for a moment saying nothing, but saying everything as our eyes worked like mediators and we released the last bit of pain that was holding us down.

"Everything is gonna be okay, Sha, I promise." I said to my brother before kissing him on the forehead and reaching over to grab my plate off the dresser.

Instead of my plate though, I grabbed the paper plate next to it which contained three pills with a note written in it.

Tisha, I'm not the bad guy and I do have a heart. But I ain't no sucker either. This time it's free, but next time you pay to play. I'm leaving two Tylenol for you and an ibuprofen for the boy. Remember, fuck with me and I will fuck with you....I'll wait though!

I read the words on the plate before quickly swiping the pills up into my hands and running them through my fingers. At that moment I felt like Eve in the Garden of Eden, holding the forbidden fruit in my hands while being tempted by the snake. I wondered whether or not those pills and the pain-free moment they offered were even worth it. I wondered if I would be able to pay as Duck said when the time came. A million thoughts ran through my mind as I sat there contemplating on what to do with the pills in my hand. After a few minutes of just sitting there looking at the pills and saying nothing, my brother Sha got tired of the wait and reached over, taking the ibuprofen out of my hand and popping it into his mouth. I watched as he swallowed it down and laid back on the pillow while looking at me.

"Just take it, Tisha. We deserve to be without pain, even if it's just for a minute." My brother said as I popped the pills into my mouth and swallowed them down with the bottled water Duck had left on the dresser.

I laid back on the small bed beside Sha after taking the pill, resting my tired aching body as my muscles in my legs and stomach tightened and my head pounded. I hoped that the relief the pill offered would be immediate as the pain in my body intensified to the point where I felt nauseous. I closed my eyes and took my brother's hand in mine as we both drifted off into a peaceful sleep. When we woke up the music had stopped to our surprise and I noticed the door to the room was open. I quickly sat up and looked around at myself and Sha trying to make sure we were okay as I wondered why someone was in the room. When I noticed the small, nine inch TV on the dresser with an Xbox next to it and a stack of books and games, I figured it was Duck because my mother had never been that nice the entire 17 years I knew her.

I woke Sha up and watched his eyes light up like it was Christmas morning when he saw all of the toys left in the room. Within minutes he was pulling his swollen, battered body up out of bed and positioning himself on the floor in front of the TV. I watched that life my brother used to have inside return to his body as he cut on the game and began playing. For the first time in my life, I felt normal in that moment, enjoying quality time with my brother in a place that wasn't filthy and where an evil tyrant wasn't lurking around the corner to beat us into submission if we didn't comply with her demands. Sha and I were in a fantasy world as we giggled, played, and enjoyed the snacks that Duck brought into the room later that day. I never felt as comfortable and relieved as I did that day even with Duck's creepy ass lurking nearby. At least I knew he cared somewhat. At least he was better than my mother.

Sha and I lived in bliss like that for two weeks. Over those two weeks my stomach got bigger as I went into my 8th week of pregnancy and Sha's physical wounds healed. We didn't notice or care about the fact that Denise had left that day and not returned. I hoped that she never came back so that one night when Duck was drunk and passed out, Sha and I could creep straight out of the front door. I knew that it would be much easier to escape with only one person watching us so having Denise gone was like a fucking holiday bonus.

The bonus I had gained in my mind was lost though on April 17th. Sha and I were lying in bed watching a movie when destruction and pain reentered our world wearing a blue sundress and flip flops. My mother like the devastating dark force that she is, came back into our world and brought with her a world of hurt and pain I would have to fight to get out of.

Chapter 5

"Uh Huh, what the fuck do we have here?"
Denise yelled as she burst into the room, taking all
of the air and peace that was inside.

Sha and I scrambled to sit up in the bed as
my heart raced and I felt light headed from getting
up so fast. Sha cowered behind me with his knees
tucked up to his chest and his forehead rested on
my back as I cradled my stomach. I held back the
tears burning behind my eyelids and the fear
brewing deep in my heart as I kept my eyes trained
on the dragon in the blue sundress standing in front
of me. I glared at my mother with deep seated
resentment fueled by years or pain and heartache
and festered into the malice I held for her very
existence. The love for her I once held on to was
completely gone because all I could see was hurt
when I looked at her.

I continued to glare at my mother as she
smirked while sucking on the Newport in her hand
before blowing smoke rings over her head. I could
feel Sha trembling behind me as Denise's voice
began to echo through the air.

"I see yo funky ass did what I said and got this house clean before I got back, you better had. But who told you muthafuckas to let the mute out. The robots told me y'all was bucking in this bitch while I was gone. Hell naw and what." My mother said as she stepped further into the room looking around me to see Sha just before the TV and games on the dresser caught her eye.

You would have thought my mother was a prize bloodhound out hunting for dinner and Bambi's juicy ass ran by when she saw the things Duck had bought us. She v-lined from the bed to the dresser quick as hell, knocking the TV down to the ground and smashing the screen. Sha whimpered behind me when he heard the TV go down and realized our fantasy world was gone. I remained strong, staring at my mother with a smirk on my face as she threw games and toys all over the floor, smashing and breaking everything in sight. I watched in amusement as my lunatic ass mother ransacked the room while raging like the fool she was, looking to evoke fear in us. Fear was what drove her and I knew that, which is why I wasn't about to give her the satisfaction.

Instead of spazzing the fuck out or crying like my mother expected me to do, I laughed in her fucking face as she broke the pink jewelry box Duck had bought for me. In that moment of defiance, I showed my mother that nothing she could do would faze me anymore. I could tell that my mother knew that too as her evil smile turned into a look of shock. For a second I thought my mother had snapped back into reality and would actually see how irrational she was being; however, when she suddenly sprinted over to the bed, jumping over me to grab Sha by the neck of his shirt, I knew that was a silly dream.

My mother's sudden movement caught me off guard as I tried to reach out and grab Sha's leg as she drug him across the bed to the floor. Before I could jump my round self up to help Sha my mother had already began unleashing a series of smacks and punches to his head and face as she cursed.

"Oh so this muthafucka bought y'all shit while I was gone like this a vacation spot, huh? Like he got money to entertain you muthafuckas, but not to give to me. Oh ok, we'll see. I bet I sale that muthafucking game. You bitches won't play that! Yo retarded ass don't deserve it anyway, neither does this tough bitch. Yo tough ass ain't gonna fold, huh Tisha? Well, I bet you fold bitch after I beat the fuck out of this dummy." My mother screamed as I ran into her, scratching her face and pulling her hair while she continued to drag a screaming Sha towards the door.

I tried to rip my mother's matted ass hair right out of her scalp as I held on to it with both hands, pulling her and my brother back deeper into the room. For a second we were in a Mexican standoff as I held on to my mother's hair and she stood doubled over holding Sha by his collar, choking him. I could hear my brother began to spit and pant for breath as my mother grunted and continued to squeeze his throat.

"I'll kill his lil ass, Tisha. You think I'm playing bitch? Let my muthafucking hair go!" Denise yelled as I ignored what she said.

Instead of listening to my mother's empty ass threats, I got a better grip of her hair with my right hand as I reached around and slipped the index finger of my left hand into her mouth, stretching her jaw. Denise screamed out in agony as I yanked her jaw and hair as hard as I could at the same time, causing her head to jerk violently to the side. I had her ass whipping from side-to-side like a rag doll in that bitch until she suddenly yelled for Duck to help her. Within seconds his instigating ass appeared, laughing before grabbing me up. I watched in horror as my mother drug Sha away face down on the dirty, hardwood floor to be locked back in the closet.

Duck held me by my waist gently as I tears rolled down my face and I screamed while trying to break free. I could hear Sha screaming my name and trying to claw his way out of the closet as Denise slammed the door shut and put a padlock on it from the outside.

"Nooo, let him out you evil bitch. LET HIM OUT PLEASE!!" I yelled to the top of my lungs as I felt the words vibrate through my body.

Sadness consumed me as I struggled to break away from Duck and get to my brother. Hearing Sha scream my name over and over again as my mother taunted him drove me crazy and fanned the flames of rage burning inside of me,

"Calm down, Tisha, calm down. I won't let her hurt you. If you say that you're my friend and one day we will play my secret game, then maybe I will help you. You better make a decision fast though because yo mammy on her way back." Duck whispered in my ear as he grinded his penis into my butt from behind.

I could hear my mother's heavy footsteps in the hall as I squirmed in Duck's arms and my heart raced a mile a minute. I knew that he was right and that in a second my mother would be right there in front of me again ready to cause me and my baby pain. That was a chance I couldn't take so I promised to give in to Satan's helper.

"Okay, okay...maybe. One day I will play your secret game with you. I promise, just please don't let her hurt me or my baby. Make her stop hurting my brother. Please, help us. I'll do whatever you want!" I said to Duck's delight as he kissed me on the tip of my ear.

I could tell that was what he had been waiting to hear as he started giggling like a school kid as he grinded my butt fast.

"I knew you would play ball eventually. I mean you can't fight the inevitable princess and you were meant to be mine. Now, let me do all the talking and shit, you just chill." Duck said as he suddenly let me go and Denise appeared in the doorway.

My mother marched right into the room with her fists clenched looking me straight in the eyes with nothing but hate. If she could have gotten to me at that moment it is no doubt in my mind that she would have beaten me to death with her bare hands, but lucky for me Duck was there. Before my mother could get to me and wrap her outstretched arms around my throat, Duck had stepped in between us and picked her up, carrying her out of the room as he cursed.

"Hell naw, Denise! Stop that shit! You gonna quit beating them damn kids all the time. You said you was about getting money bitch, not beating them. Ole dumb ass hoe, then you broke all the shit I bought. Bitch is you crazy? I guess I gotta teach yo stupid ass a lesson, huh?" Duck yelled at my mother as he drug her down the hall.

I felt the walls shake as he slammed her into their bedroom door before pushing her inside. Screams and the sounds of his fists hitting her flesh were all I heard for the ten minutes following as I crouched down in the hallway, talking to my brother through a crack in the door. When Denise's screams finally stopped, I was able to sneak back into the room without being seen. I sat there for hours listening to my brother talk through the vent we discovered connected the closet to the room, and waiting on whatever disaster that was coming next.

To my surprise hours went past and nothing happened. I didn't even hear my mother's voice again until well after nine that night when Duck's nephew Fat came over to visit and serve my mother crack. He was a tall, fat, light skinned boy with freckles all over his face and long dreads. He looked familiar to me, like one of the boys in Terricka's gang, but I wasn't sure as I walked into the living room to see why Duck had called me.

"Aye Tish, this my nephew Fat. He a real nigga you should holler at him instead of the nothing ass nigga who got you pregnant and disappeared. Anyway, its food and shit in here, you can eat and you can take your brother something. Denise stupid ass ain't gonna fuck with ya. Ain't that right, bitch?" Duck asked as he turned his head to the side like he was talking to the imaginary person standing behind the couch.

Just then my mother stood up with a pipe in her hand, nothing on but a black g-string and black, leather dog collar, with a totally sprung expression on her battered face. Her right eye was completely swollen shut and she had bruises and cuts all over her caramel skin, but none of that stopped her from being as repulsive as possible. I thought I was in a scene straight out of New Jack City or The Wire as she took a big hit off the crack pipe, deeply inhaling and holding the thick white smoke before blowing it all out in a thin, faint line. She looked like a true cone, cracked out, prostitute as she stood there bucking her eyes at me while she continued to take long hits off the pipe before answering.

"Yeah, that's right daddy. I ain't gonna fuck with them…right now." My mother mumbled quickly before holding out her hand to Duck.

I watched as Duck placed one 20 piece of rock in her palm before dismissing her to their room as he stood up smiling.

"See I got that hoe trained. I told you, I'm in control. Not that junky bitch. Now, chill with my nephew while I go handle this." Duck said before flipping my hair with his hand and blowing an air kiss at me.

I held in my disgust and faked a small smile back at him before he disappeared down the hall, leaving me sitting there on the couch with his nephew. For a while we just sat there, saying nothing as we stared at the basketball game on TV. When the game went on its fourth commercial the boy finally spoke and began the conversation that would spark a new fire. After a little small talk I found out the apartments we were in was called the Peach Tree and that I was right across the street from The Overlook apartments where Terricka and her gang was. After a little more talking, I found out Fat was folk and that he knew my sister personally, so I pulled the gang's loyalty card and made him promise that he would find my sister and tell her where I was.

After my conversation with Fat, I felt a new found confidence and bravery so when Duck came back into the room I demanded my brother be let out to eat. My demand worked too because before I knew it Duck had went into his room and returned with the key, letting Sha out to eat in the living room with everyone else like a human. I hugged my brother and told him how much I loved him the entire time we ate, not taking my eye off of him for a second. After dinner I convinced Duck to let Sha take a bath and sleep in the same room as me.

"Oh you gonna owe me big time, Tisha." Duck said as he licked his tongue out to me while standing in the doorway of the room I slept in.

I rolled my eyes at Duck as I lie there in the bed with Sha curled up behind me while I staring at his nasty ass do flicking motions with his tongue. All the while his nephew Fat, stood in the

91

doorway behind him, looking at me with sympathy and compassion. I played on Fat's soft heart at that moment, winking my eye to indicate I was depending on him. I watched Fat nod his head before I turned away so that Duck's bullshit would stop. After a few seconds Duck finally got the picture and saw that I wasn't turning back around so he laughed and taunted me as he slowly closed the door.

"Yeaaaa…Tisha my Tisha. I got you!" Duck whispered before slamming the door and sealing my future fate.

I breathed a breath of relief when Duck left the room; however, I knew that I would have to deal with him and answer to the promise I made one day. I just hoped that when that time came, I would be ready.

Chapter 6

The next day, April 18th and my sister Terricka's 18th birthday, I heard nothing from her or Fat for that matter. I paced the floor and drove myself crazy wondering where she was all day, hoping that she would be able to help us. I waited, I prayed, and I wished my sister a happy birthday over and over again as I stared out of the small window that my mother had boarded up from the inside; however, my sister never came. Two more days went by in a blur as I waited on my sister and her homies to rescue us while watching my mother regain her evil composure. By then my mother had already began her reign of terror on me and Sha again, refusing to let us eat or sleep. It seemed Duck's powers were gone and so was he for the most part, leaving Sha and I to face evil alone, and evil is exactly what my mother was.

Denise was like a possessed alley cat in our faces every second of the day trying to inflict pain on us. The only relief we got was when Duck came back that day and told my mother he had a lick downtown that would bring them lots of money. My mother had both me and Sha kneeling in rice on the kitchen floor, holding five books in each hand while she sliced us across the back with a leather belt when Duck bust into the house. From the look on Duck's face when he came in, I could tell that even though he was fucked up in his own way he still had a conscious. The disgusted expression on his face when he saw our bloody backs and heard our moans of agony, told me that he didn't like what my mother did to us. I think that is why he did what he did to get my mother out of the house and away from us. Beneath that pedophile, sadist exterior there was a nice man somewhere inside of Duck, and that was lucky for us.

"Maine what the fuck you got going, Denise? Come on now, you said you was gonna cut that shit out. Let them kids the fuck up and let's go get this money. We can go get some dope when we finish." Duck said walking into the kitchen and winking his eye at me before grabbing my mother by the hand and pulling her to the door.

Hearing a promise of money and drugs was all my mother needed to hear to distract her. Duck's news instantly put my mother's junky, greedy ass in the best mood ever as she let Duck guide her out of the room, leaving me and Sha alone to go get dressed. However, neither Sha nor I had the strength or indignation necessary to pull ourselves up and fight evil at that moment. We both remained on our knees, holding our breath, just waiting on our hell to end until Duck came back into the kitchen and told us to get up.

"Maine, y'all get the fuck up off that floor. I'm taking her downtown for a few hours, but I ain't coming back with her. Be in the room quiet, preferably sleep when she comes back and you should be okay. Now, smile my princess. Duck gonna take care of you remember? Remember our deal too. Okay?" Duck said nudging my chin with his knuckle before smiling and blowing a kiss at me.

I swallowed down my screams and anxiety as I let Duck help me to my feet and then pulled my brother up beside me. Sha clung to me as we stood there watching Duck while he looked me up and down, licking his lips and rubbing his hands together. After a few seconds of staring at one another, we all suddenly stopped and looked towards the hallway as the sound of my mother dragging feet across the hardwood floor on her way to the door echoed through the air. I could feel the hair on the back of my neck stand up as she yelled and screamed curses from the door.

"Come the fuck on Duck, while you in there in that lil slut fucking face." My mother spat like venom before stepping into the kitchen to look at me as she spoke.

"Oh yea, lil bitch don't think I forgot. We got something to discuss tonight because I need my first fucking payment. This maid shit ain't paying the fucking bills or helping me the fuck out so its time yo funky ass get with it...and you WILL get with it. Now, I want the retard back in his hole by the time I get back and yo funky ass better be done cleaned up, washed yo ass, and be in there waiting on me. I mean it, Tisha, and remember... they watching." My mother said while looking up at the ceiling as she reached her arm out to grab my shoulder and I stepped out of her reach.

I pushed Sha behind me and glared at my mother with malice as she stood in the door to the kitchen looking at me and smiling. After a few seconds, Duck came and grabbed my mother by the arm, pulling her to the door as he winked his eye at me. I rolled my eyes at him as I smirked at my mother while she struggled in Duck's arms trying to break free to get to me.

"Lil bitch, I don't see what the fuck you smiling for. I'll come smack that smirk right off yo fucking face. Silly ass Hiefa!" My mother yelled as she held on to the door jam and Duck tried to pull her out.

"Oh. And don't try to get away either, Tisha. The doors and windows are padlocked and I have people all around the apartments watching for me. Try me if you wonna, bitch. There is no escape so just don't try it because you know what will happen when I find you. Just wait until I find yo funky ass sister and you will see. Remember what I said…they watching!" My mother yelled as Duck pushed her on out of the front door.

As soon as the door slammed shut behind them, I felt instant relief as I ran to the door and put my ear to it, listening to the three deadbolts being locked and then a padlock being put on the door from the outside. I turned around to see a terrified yet angry expression on Sha's face as I tried to hide the fear and malice surging through me. I manage a weak smile at my brother as he walked over to the door and stood beside me before speaking.

"   We ain't gonna never escape this hell, are we Tisha?" Sha asked me as I looked at him and saw the defeated look I once had now consuming him.

I could do nothing but cry as I pulled my brother close to me and hugged him. I couldn't answer his question because I didn't know if we would ever escape. The only thing I did know was that I wouldn't stop trying no matter what. After that I fixed Sha and I a good meal, cleaned the house, showered, and prepared for the horror that was to come. I tried to devise a safe way for Sha and I to escape from the third story kitchen window, over the parking lot after working on opening the front door, but no matter what I did I saw no safe way out, if any way at all. At about 11:30 p.m. I fell out in bed next to Sha, exhausted and hurting all over. I dreamed about Jerrod and I living a happy life and I could feel his love all over me.

In my dream Jerrod ran his hands all over my stomach and covered the skin on my growing belly with his loving kisses. My dream felt so real that when I woke up my first instinct was to reach out for him, even before I opened my eyes. When I did reach out and actually touched someone's face, I almost jumped out of the bed. I quickly opened my eyes and focused them on the person sitting in front of me on the bed as my heart raced and I pressed my body up against Sha's, pinning him against the wall.

I pulled my gown down with shaky hands as I stared around the dimly lit room quickly before focusing on the person in front of me again. When my eyes fully focused, I noticed there was a young mixed man, about 24 or 25 with a big nappy afro, huge glasses, and pimples all over his face, sitting there smiling at me. He was so creepy looking just sitting there with his hands stretched out towards me and his lips still puckered from when he was kissing my stomach. The whole Twilight Zone ass scene caught me off guard leaving nothing more for me to do other than scream.

I screamed long and hard as the creepy little bastard still sitting on the bed tried to shush me and I kicked his ass with all of my might. One of my wild kicks hit him on the tip of his penis which was protruding through the tight Levis jeans he had on. That kick was enough to send his ass jolting up from the bed like he had touched a hot stove. In an instant he was on his feet and backing towards the door as I yelled for his perverted ass to get out and Sha slowly woke up out of his coma while calling my name.

"Tisha, what's going on? What's wrong?" Sha asked as he ground the sleep out of his eyes with his fists and I cried while covering myself in the covers.

I yelled for Sha to get back as I wrapped the sheet around myself and reached for the six inch piece of wood with nails sticking out of it I had on the floor next to the bed. After I couldn't find a way to escape the day before, I broke a piece of the wood off of the window to use as weapon if I needed it. From the looks of the muthafucka in the room when I woke up, I definitely needed it then and for some reason I wasn't scared to use it.

Sha jumped out of bed quickly and cowered down in the corner as I held the piece of wood in my hand like I was a batter ready to swing. I huffed and spat like a demon as I hurled curses at the stunned pervert ready to beat the fuck out of him if I had to. For a second I felt enraged and out of control like my mother and sister often got, and it felt good.

"Come on muthafucka, touch me again. I want you to put yo muthafucking hands on me you perverted bitch and I'm about to body yo ass. I'M TIRED OF THIS BULLSHIT. GETTTT OUTTTTT!!!!" I yelled to the top of my lungs as I began swinging the piece of wood wildly in the air.

I could hear the young pervert grunting and whimpering as I popped his creepy ass across the forearm with one of my wild swings. I didn't give a fuck though. I kept my eyes closed tightly as I continued to swing the wood, releasing years of being tired of being scared and being tired in general. I cried and popped the creep repeatedly on the arms and head before suddenly the door to the room swung open and all of the air left my body once again.

I stood there frozen with the piece of wood in my hands as I looked at my mother standing in the doorway asshole naked with a pair of white usher gloves on, white orthopedic heels, pearls, teacher's glasses, and her hair brushed into a tight, high bun. It was the creepiest, most sadistically, perverse shit I had ever seen before in my life, and nothing my mother ever did shocked me anymore. However, as she walked into the room with her head held high smelling like Ivory soap, all clean and shit with a ruler in her hand, I knew she was on her worse behavior. That's why I backed up against the wall with my stick still in hand ready to fuck her up if I had to. At that moment I was sure I would have to, eventually.

My heart raced in my chest as I watched my mother walk into the room hitting the ruler in the palm of her hand as the 2 inch heels of her orthopedic shoes clacked on the hardwood floor. The sound of my mother's laugh and the clack of her shoes made my flesh crawl like someone scratching a chalkboard as I backed into the wall at the foot of the bed, keeping my eye on my brother cowered down at the head of the bed near the door. I tried hard to swallow down the fear and huge lump in my throat as I watched my mother motion for the young pervert to come to her.

"Oh come here Joshua what happened to you." My mother asked the creep in a calm, motherly almost saintly voice as she inspected his wounds.

I watched as my mother kissed each one of his gashes and then ran her fingers through his hair as she hummed. My mind reeled as I watched the creep quiver and whimper at my mother's warm touch which quickly turned perverse as she French kissed him while grabbing his crouch. I quickly looked away and glanced over to see my brother tucked into a perfect little ball, almost under the head of the bed. I wished at that second that I could curl up into a ball and become invisible just like Sha as I glanced back over at my mother to see her glaring at me. Her expression was so eerily calm it took me completely by surprise as I looked into her glossy eyes and she once again tried to persuade me into doing what she wanted.

"Now Tisha, I told you we were going to have a discussion. Didn't I? I told you that you would have to pull your weight. Didn't I?" My mother asked me as she walked closer to me, so close that I could feel the spit as it flew off of her lips.

I felt my body tremble slightly as my mother put her face so close to mine I could smell the alcohol, heroin, cocaine, and everything else she had consumed coming out of her pores. I made my body stiff and looked straight ahead as my mother stared into my eyes with an insane look and shoulder bumped me, trying to use intimidation. She was trying the scare tactics she had used all of my life. The only difference was that shit wasn't working anymore. I wasn't the same weak, naive, vulnerable victim I had been all of my life.

Gone were the days I was just going to sit by idly and let her torture me. What my mother didn't know was that I had someone growing inside of me I was willing to fight for and that made me way more dangerous than her. I just had to be pushed to it. I glared back at my mother with so much anger she had to blink and look away for a second before continuing her rant. Even with Denise yelling, cursing, and spitting in my face though, I still looked her dead in the eyes and held on to my stick, keeping her back away from me.

"So, tell me why the fuck are you not in here sucking and rubbing Joshua into ecstasy? I made it easier on you, Tisha. Don't embarrass me in front of clients. Do what you are told?" My mother whispered to me in a calm, but cold voice through clenched teeth.

I astonished myself as I shook my head no and stretched my arms out, suddenly pushing my mother in her chest keeping her away from me. My impromptu act of bravery took her totally by surprise too because it was written all over her face as she smacked her lips and rolled her head. The devious, vengeful look in my mother's eyes as she stepped up to me again, bumping my shoulder as I bumped her back, let me know that I was in for a hell of a fight. However, the way I stood firm and mean mugged my mother, giving her just as much hate as she gave out, let her know that I would not be an easy target. It was like the clash of the titans as we both stared each other down, breathing hard, and emitting fumes of anger and hate. My mother was the first to break our stare off as she laughed before leaning in to whisper to me.

"You'll be sorry for embarrassing me like this little bitch. I've told you before, I RUN THIS! You ain't got yo sister around to help no more bitch so it's all on you. You will do what I say or else, Tisha. Mark my words. Be ready for war when I get back bitch!" My mother said in my face through clenched teeth before laughing hysterically.

I covered my ears with my hands to block out the sound of her voice as I watched her wave Joshua out of the room before she turned back to me.

"Go wait on me in the other room, Joshua, I'll take care of you and give you a discount for Tisha in the future. Just wait on me in there." My mother said as Joshua smiled at her while rubbing his hands together like a greedy crook.

I looked away when he glared at me and smirked on his way out of the door. As soon as Joshua stepped into the hallway, I looked back in my mother's direction as she stepped towards the door. As my mother stepped into the hallway, she suddenly dashed back into the room and over towards the bed, grabbing Sha up in his collar. She grabbed him and drug him out into the hallway so fast, closing the door and locking it behind her, I didn't even have a chance to move my feet. By the time I made it to the door and began banging on it with my stick I could hear Sha screaming followed by the sound of him being thrown in the closet and the door slamming shut behind him.

"Let him go you bitch. I hate you Denise you rotten ass monster!" I yelled to the top of my lungs as I beat on the door with all of my might.

I felt my anger rise even more as my mother laughed at my rage from the other side of the door, taunting me like she always did.

"Shut the fuck up, Shartisha! You brought this shit on yourself and your mute ass brother. If you would have only done what the fuck I said we wouldn't be going through this. But NOOOO, you tough, so suffer for a while bitch. When I come back though, Tisha, it's on! One way or the other bitch. Don't believe me just watch." My mother said before she walked away with her wicked ass laugh trailing behind her.

I shook off the anger and twinge of fear her laugh brought as worry about Sha began to take over me. I couldn't help but to freak out as I suddenly realized he was completely quiet.

"SHA ARE YOU ALRIGHT?" I screamed hysterically as I beat on the wall next to the vent, waiting on Sha to answer me.

After a few seconds, I could hear my brother breathing hard next to the vent before speaking up to comfort my fears.

"I'm okay, Tisha. All she did was punch me in the mouth. I've gotten those since I was about one so that's nothing. You just have to calm down. Think about the baby, Tisha. We're good for now and maybe Fat will find Terricka and she'll come. We just have to keep from crashing out until then, Tish. Okay?" Sha said to me as I cried, groaned, and raged, beating and pushing on the wall trying to take all of my frustrations out on it.

I was so consumed by my emotions at that moment I barley saw or heard anything around me. However, when I remembered and really thought about what Sha had just said, I couldn't do anything but laugh through my tears after hearing such wisdom coming from someone so young. I knew that Sha was right. I knew that in such a situation the sensible thing would be for me to just hold on and keep my cool. However, what I didn't tell Sha was how I could feel something bad coming. I didn't tell him how I saw death in my dreams and how I knew the only way I could protect us all was by fighting. I couldn't tell Sha why I had to do whatever it took to get him out, I just had to do it and that's exactly what I planned on doing.

"Okay little brother. I'll go to sleep but you do the same, promise me." I said to my brother as I wiped away my tears before leaning my head on the wall next to the vent.

I could hear Sha sucking up his tears and laying down on the floor as I pressed my face closer to the wall.

"Okay Tisha, I will. Love you big sister, always. Without you I don't know what I would do. That's why no matter what I will always love you, look out for you, and never leave your side.

No Matter what! Goodnight Tish." Sha said as tears just poured out of my eyes like faucets with no warning.

I had to hold my mouth to force back my cries as I felt my brother's love pour through the 8 inches of plaster that separated us. I kissed the wall and told Sha how much I loved him back, sending just as much love back through the thin sheetrock.

"I love you to the moon and back little brother. Just like uncle Scooby used to tell me. My love for you has no limits just like that and don't you ever forget that Sha. Now go to sleep pumpkin head because our better days are coming." I said to my brother through the vent as I stepped away from the wall and walked over to look at myself in the mirror over the small dresser.

I looked like I aged five years in five days as I glared at the stress lines all over my face while wiping away my tears.

"Better days are coming, one way or another. Maybe I'll have to slay a fucking dragon or two in order to get to my happily ever after. Oh well, fuck those dragons. I deserve happiness, so I'll be ready for whatever when the time comes. Yeah, I'm ready Denise. Fuck it, it's me or you!" I said to myself as I sat my stick on the dresser and laid on the concrete like bed, staring up at the ceiling thinking about the battle to come.

Chapter 7

For five days following my face off with the creep and Denise I prepared physically and mentally for an epic battle. I heard Denise leave the house that first day and didn't return so with Duck nowhere in sight Sha and I were locked in our separate prisons all alone. I spent that first day and the next, crying and talking to my brother through the vent as he complained about being hungry. I understood the hunger pains he complained of and the headaches that were constant and often overpowering. By day three, April 23rd, all of the sadness and fear I had developed from the lack of food and worry over what would happen to us was totally replaced with the anger I had before. I paced the floor going over kill moves in my mind as I swung my stick wildly in the air.

"No more, sitting duck, cry baby, pussy bullshit, I'm sick of it. Denise think she got me spooked but she got me fucked up. Ain't no hoe in my blood, she should know that. I guess it's time I show her. I'M GETTING US OUT OF HERE SHA. I PROMISE!!" I screamed as something

112

shiny poking from behind the raggedy dresser caught my eye.

I listened for Sha's response as I scurried over to the dresser and ripped the long piece of metal that helped to hold the mirror to the bottom of the dresser off. The thick, cold piece of steel was barely hanging on so it was easy for me to snatch it off, turning it in my hands trying to get a feel of it. The piece of metal had some good weight and a nice length on it, which made it the perfect weapon to smack someone with and get the fuck back in time to strike again. I knew that it would be a very useful tool if I had to face my mother drugged out to the max and mad; however, I still wasn't confident it was enough.

I knew that if my mother was mad enough and on enough drugs she could fight a fucking polar bear. Hell, once when I was eight I saw her fight three mall security guards while she was off her meds and high on a three day crack binge. She was like the Incredible Hulk on their asses throwing them and shit. They say cocaine is a powerful drug and from the way it made my mother a fucking psychotic, savage I knew that shit was true and that I needed more. That's why my next thought was to sharpen the pointy end of the metal on the concrete windowsill as I waited on my fate.

As I ran the pointy edge of the metal along the concrete windowsill forming a sharp side, and pointy edge, I imagined a bloody, gruesome battle with my mother in which I lost my baby and my own life. I saw everything go down and although I lost in the end I took Denise's evil ass with me and accomplished my goal of ensuring that both my brother and sister were free.

In my mind I saw them walk away in the sunset, hand-in-hand so I felt at peace in that moment even if that meant I had to die. At least my baby and I would be together away from all of the pain. I figured we didn't have Jerrod anyway, so why hold on. Thoughts of him laying somewhere dead had crossed my mind so often I had to remember his smile, his smell, and his touch to drown it out. I didn't want to live without him so giving up to save my siblings seemed like the best thing to do.

I smiled as I imagined Jerrod's handsome face and felt his arms wrapped around me, cradling the tiny piece of us growing inside of me. It felt so real as his love filled me with warmth and I suddenly felt tears streaming down my face. I wiped away the tears that were falling from my eyes as Sha spoke abruptly and shook me out of my sudden sadness.

"I wonna get out of here as much as you do, Tisha, but I don't wonna lose you to do it. I know you're tired. I know you're fed up with all this bullshit, but one thing I know is it can't last forever. Something has to give. Let's just stay strong together big sis. I love you, Tisha. Sing me that song I heard you working on yesterday." Sha said as I suddenly stopped sharpening the metal and looked toward the vent.

I was surprised because I didn't think he heard me singing my heart out through my tears in the middle of the night. I didn't think anyone heard me talking to God, crying out for help, and channeling my sister's defiant strength. That night I wrote a song for both of us taking on both personalities and both roles. For a moment I was both Tisha and Terricka, or wind and fire, as my uncle Scooby would say. I sang and rapped all of my pain out and gained the strength I needed to turn that sadness into anger. That song helped to transform me into the Tisha, who was willing to fight for what she believed in. That song was my new muse.

"Sing the song, Tisha..Please!" Sha said as I sat the metal down and walked over to the vent, putting my back on the wall and sliding down to the floor.

I swallowed down the lump in my throat as I stared up at the ceiling, visualizing my words in the form of flashes of scenes from my life. I saw all of the pain my sister, brother, and I went through, but I also saw those who loved and helped us along the way. Imagining the loving faces of Mrs. Cunningham, The Robinson's, Jerrod, and his mother, and even Lisa, although she had abandoned us because of the sins of our mother like everyone else, helped me to push through my emotions to sing the song. I was able to slow my breathing and stop my heart from racing long enough to visualize the words to the song as my brother encouraged me from behind the wall.

"Take your time and sing it, Tisha." My brother said, encouraging me as I swallowed hard and channeled my sister's strength again.

I could feel that Terricka fire in my stomach, pushing me to say what was on my mind and in my heart regardless of who liked it.

"Let that shit out lil sis, fuck how it turn out!" I could hear my big sister's voice ringing in my ears.

For a second it felt as if Terricka was right there with me and we were back in the bed with blood in our panties, crying our eyes out as we poured our emotions out in a song. I could feel my sister's love and resilience inside of me and hear my brother's confidence through the wall. Suddenly, my emotions burst forward and the rap to the song I wrote just came flowing out of me without warning. My voice was so strong, confident, and firm, I almost didn't recognize it myself as I took on Terricka's part.

"People telling me that hard times can't last forever,

But I wonder how they'd feel if shit never got better.

I wonder just how they'd survive if day after day they felt pain,

Bet they'd crash the fuck out, blow their brains out, cause we ain't the same.

I'm slowly realizing the fact that I was built for this shit,

My mama might be a psycho junky but she ain't raise no bitch.

I'm a shooter beneath the sadness, a beast on the loose,

Cause I'm sick and tired of the anguish and the fucking abuse.

It's time to flip this shit and click, unleash what's brewing inside,

See I'm hunting for all of my demons and there's nowhere to hide.

The day of reckoning has come and facing my wrath no one wins,

No more passing off your burdens, answer for yo own sins!"

I rapped with so much emotion I didn't even realize that I was crying until I felt the warm tears as they fell down the front of my shirt. I quickly wiped them away with the back of my hand before swallowing down that lingering sadness and replacing it with strength. When I began singing the chorus to the song, my voice came out even stronger and clearer as I gained the additional strength I needed to face the evil to come.

"See I got my crosses, I can't carry yours no more,

(No More)

I got my life to live and it's worth fight for.

I spent so many years fighting a battle I couldn't win,

But that shit's over, I'm giving you back the burden of yo sins!"

I sang as I felt a level of fortitude I never knew that I had, grow inside of me. I felt like I could conquer the world as the words to the song echoed in my ears. I pulled myself up off the floor and pressed my head against the vent as Sha expressed his feelings about the song to me.

"Tisha, maine that was hot. I felt that sis. I felt like you and Terricka were in there together like old times and I was in my room, locked away from mama with my ear to the wall listening. I'm happy you have your music to get you through, Tisha. And I'm glad that I have you." Sha said as I felt tears well up in my eyes.

As Sha's words rang in my ears, I fought the urge to cry and let sadness or any weak emotions invade my body at that time. I knew that I needed to keep my mind clear and stay strong for the battle that was sure to come. I had to keep my kill or be killed mentality intact until the war was over, and that's what I did.

"I love you lil bruh, til the end of the earth and back. You always got me. Now, go to sleep. Hopefully Duck will come soon and he'll let us out to eat. Just hold on. I told you, I got you." I said to Sha as I rubbed the wall next to the vent before stepping away.

As I walked across the room and sat on the concrete-like bed, my stomach growled so loudly it sounded like an angry lion was in the room. I laid back and rubbed the small bulge with a tiny fetus growing inside, comforting and soothing one of the only people I had in my life who would love me.

"It's okay little baby, we'll get food soon. Everything is going to be okay. Be strong. You are me and you are your father so you have no choice but to be strong my son. I know you're a boy with a smile just like your father's and those beautiful eyes. I love you my child. I love you to the moon and back and I will never let anything happen to you. Daddy will be home soon. He'll save us. Just hold on baby. Just hold on." I whispered to my baby as I felt my eye lids grow so heavy I couldn't keep them open.

Sleep hit me hard and sudden as I fell into a coma-like state with visions of Jerrod playing in my head. I dreamed of our reunion and the happy life we would have with our son once our nightmare was over. I saw our entire lives flash before my eyes and for once in my dreams there was the happiness I always wanted. However, there was one thing that made my heart race in my sleep and caused me to toss and turn on the hard bed. That horrifying reality was the fact that my brother and sister were nowhere in sight. In my dreams I had created a fairytale life with my husband and kids, yet the brother and sister I loved dearly were not there.

That made me realize subconsciously that their sunset and happily ever after I saw in my daydream wasn't the same as mine. The harsh reality of a fact I knew deep down inside hit me hard even in my sleep. I jumped up out of the bed suddenly, swinging my arms wildly and screaming my sister and brother's name after seeing a vision of my wedding with neither one of them there. I couldn't stop my heart from racing madly or slow my breathing as I focused my eyes and glanced around the room. The first thing that I noticed when I was able to focus my eyes was that the door to the room was open.

I quickly straightened my gown and crept towards the open door on my tip toes as my heart beat wildly and I felt light headed. I could hear muffled voices coming from the living room as I made it into the door way, which caused me to double back to grab my stick off the dresser before peeking out into the hall. I glanced quickly from side-to-side, peering down the hallway before slipping over to the closet Sha was kept locked in.

I was shocked when I went to reach for the knob and found that the door was already open. I called out for Sha in the darkness as I crouched down and stepped into the closet but I quickly discovered he wasn't inside. I felt my legs wobble beneath me as I made my way out of the dark, stinky, cramped closet and back into the semi-fresh air of the hallway.

I breathed in deeply as I put my back against the wall and crept down the hall towards the living room. I kept the stick gripped firmly in my hand ready to strike as I neared the door way to the living room. I held my breath as squeezed my eyes tightly shut and thought about getting me and my brother free. Any apprehension I had lurking inside of me quickly dissipated as I stepped around the corner to face what I thought would be an epic battle with the monster from my nightmares. However, when I stepped into the living room all that I saw was a still semi-clean room in which my clean and happy brother was laying on the floor besides Duck playing the Xbox. I couldn't help but to stand there with my mouth open, ready to catch flies as I watched my brother giggle at Duck's joke before suddenly noticing me and jumping to his feet.

"Tisha, you're finally awake. I wanted to wake you up, but Duck told me to let you sleep. Come on, Duck brought us new clothes, food, a new game, and he said we can stay out until mama come back on Friday night. That's two days, Tisha, we can be out. Be happy, Tisha." My brother squealed threw his excitement as he ran over to me and hugged me tightly.

I hugged Sha back as I glared at Duck while he smiled back at me. Although I was grateful for the bit of kindness he did show me and my brother, I still remembered who he was and I knew that eventually the kindness would wear off. Somehow I knew that as soon as the time came and he didn't get what he wanted, the true him would show. Despite all of the kind gestures, I could feel that beneath that smile there was malice and a perverted man waiting to prey on the weak. He had me fucked up though. I wasn't going to be the easy target I had been with Jerome. I would fuck a nigga up if he thought he was just going to take something from me again.

I couldn't help but to giggle as I stood there mean mugging Duck and a vision of me giving his ugly ass a chemical peel with battery acid flashed before my eyes. I had to quickly wipe the grin off my face though when I noticed Duck looking at me.

"Yeah baby girl, be happy like Sha said. Duck took care of y'all like always. Now, go wash up and shit then eat. I'm going out for a while but I'll be back tonight. Don't worry your mama won't be home for two more days. Y'all can eat and kick it until then, but Friday afternoon y'all gotta go back before she get here. I'm gonna stash some food in y'all rooms so when she lock y'all back up y'all will be straight. I gotcha. I can make shit even better though, Tisha, remember that." Duck said as I glared at him and he winked before darting around the corner and out of the front door.

I waited until I heard Duck lock all of the deadbolts and put the padlock on before I hugged my brother and began searching the house frantically for a way out and weapons. After about 20 minutes of trying to get out to no avail, I gave up on that plan again and began looking for tools to defend myself. By the time my search was over I had found a small pocket knife, a strong piece of wire, and a fake pregnant belly my mother used for boosting.

I quickly took the things I found into the room and stashed them under the thin mattress to serve as my weapons and armor for my impending battle. Once I had my tools secure I returned to the living room to get the pink juicy pajama set Duck had brought me and went to take a shower. I felt a ton of worry and stress leave my body as I stood in the shower and let the hot water pour down on me. I almost felt normal and like I had a real life as I enjoyed the simple pleasure of getting clean.

After my shower, I joined Sha in the living room where we ate pizza, tacos, and KFC chicken until we were blue in the face. Sometime later both Sha and I passed out on the couch with a chicken bucket between us and smiles on our faces as Crooklyn played on the small TV.

Chapter 8

I awoke to Duck nudging my shoulder as he escorted a skinny, 20-something light skinned female, with long red weave, and a big ghetto booty down the hall to his and my mother's room. I looked up and rolled my eyes at Duck as he tried to block my view of the girl before putting on his good nigga act.

"Oh hey baby girl. Get up and go to bed now. You and Sha can both sleep together. No worries Duck here. I'm fina let my, uhhh, cousin sleep off her drunk in our room. Y'all gone lay down now." Duck said as I glared at him through sleepy eyes.

I really didn't give a fuck what he did, especially to my mother, but the fact that he thought he was fooling me did have me salty as fuck. I shook Sha awake before helping him to his feet as Duck stood in the doorway watching us. When we made it to the room, I was kept in Duck stopped me at the door as I urged Sha to go on in and lay down.

"Aye Tisha, I don't have to say that what happens when we here stays between us, do I? Not after all the rules I've broken for you. I know you mad and shit because I held you for Denise but when faced with doing what she wants me to or helping you, I gotta pick her. I fuck with you though and I'll fuck with you more as soon as you play ball. You'll see. You gotta be nice though. I know you don't want all the good shit happening for you and yo brother to run out. So think about that princess and keep yo fucking mouth closed." Duck said to me calmly through clenched teeth as he leaned in close to my face.

I held my breath and stood there still, not even looking at his weak ass as he continued to glare at me. After a few seconds, he laughed and kissed me on the cheek before disappearing down the hall. I quickly went into the room fuming, wishing I had stabbed Duck in the neck with the pocket knife I had stashed up my coochie. I quickly removed the knife and stashed it under my side of the mattress before getting in bed, beside Sha. He laid with his back to me facing the wall trying to pretend like he was asleep as I deeply exhaled the tension I was holding inside.

"Tisha and the Blow Fish, huh?" Sha suddenly said as we both broke out into hysterical laughter.

I tickled my brother for a while and we wrestled in the hard bed, carefree and for the first time in a long time happy. Our happiness lasted until that Friday too with Duck keeping his promise and surprising us with another movie and take-out night before a day of games. I did my best to ignore Duck's advances and all of the long stares and shit during the fun times. However, the rage burning inside of me grew stronger each second I was around him. By the time Friday rolled around and my mother was expected to return home, I felt like I was about to bust with emotions. I had so much trapped anger, anxiety, fear, and hurt built up inside of me I was anxious to unleash it on someone, anyone. I didn't have to wait long for that opportunity though because at about 8 a.m. that morning Duck woke me and Sha up suddenly and told Sha to go back to his closet.

"Aye, y'all get up and go back to the way y'all was, Denise will be here sooner than I thought. Sha there's food in there and shit you gone be straight. Gone get yo hugs and shit so you can roll homie." Duck said to Sha firmly as my confused little brother sat up in the bed beside me, rubbing sleep out of his eyes.

I quickly hugged Sha close to me and kissed his forehead before pushing him out of the bed and towards the door. When Sha got into the hallway, he stopped to look at me before speaking and when our eyes met I read his mind.

"Be safe, Tisha. I love you!" My brother said as I whispered the words, "I love you" back and he disappeared next door with Duck.

I stood there listening as Duck locked Sha back in the closet before coming to lock me in my own prison. As soon as the door closed, I began my preparation, strapping the pregnant belly my mother used to shoplift over my little belly and then stuffing my flat pillow inside for extra coverage. I then got my pocket knife out and stuck it back up my vajayjay before placing the wire inside the small fold on the headboard. Once I was sure all of my weapons were securely hidden, I stood in the middle of the floor with my stick and sharpened piece of metal in hand, looking at myself in the mirror as I did kill moves. I mentally prepared myself for what was to come, hoping I would have the courage necessary to slay the dragon.

"I'm ready…As tired as I am, I can't be nothing but ready. The question is, is she?" I asked myself as I looked in the mirror and acted out killing my mother by slicing her neck with the piece of sharpened metal.

The Tisha I saw staring back at me when I looked in the mirror made the hair on my neck stand up. I almost didn't recognize myself with the deranged grin I was sporting. I knew right then I was more like my mother than I'd ever admit. However, I knew that was exactly what I needed to defeat her. I knew that I had to meet crazy with crazy, and I was ready.

I stood behind the door to my prison for hours with the piece of wood in my hands, the metal sticking down my pajama leg, and a pocket knife up my cooch. I was suited and booted, ready for battle the second my mother walked in.

At around eleven thirty that morning, I got exactly what I had been waiting for as I sat on the floor behind the door with my stick in my hands. As soon as I heard the front door fly open, I knew it was Denise from the way my heart started racing and the hair all over my body stood up. I got to my feet in a hurry as the sound of my mother huffing and puffing followed by the heavy pound of her naked feet on the hardwood floor filled the air.

I fought to keep my cool as the sound of my mother's furious voice vibrated through the air, into my body, piercing my soul.

"Yeah bitch, I'm on my way….. I told yo funky ass." My mother said through clenched teeth as she marched towards me like a tsunami.

At that moment fear tried to creep back in and make me a slave of my mother's insanity once again. However, I was too mad and fed up to be afraid. I just wanted it all to be over with and I was ready to get it done by any means necessary. I got into the perfect batters stance behind the door as Denise continued to curse while unlocking the padlock on the outside. I don't know what my mother expected when she barged into the room that morning, but from the way she walked right into the nail end of my stick as soon as she came through the door told me that she didn't expect me to fight back.

Somehow my mother expected me to just lay there and let her do whatever she wanted to do to me after all I had been through. That was what she wanted but she got the exact opposite as I hit her with everything I had two good times in the face with the stick before she knocked it out of my hands. I could hear the flesh on her cheek and forehead ripping as she knocked the stick to the ground and I punched her repeatedly in the head. I tried to jump back and pull my metal out of my pajama leg fast but my mother recovered from the blows to the face faster than I anticipated. Before I knew it, she was rushing me with blood pouring out of her wounds and wrapping her hand in my hair.

My mother tried to pound me in the face as she held my hair, but the fight in me just wouldn't let it go down like that. I quickly got a burst of energy, despite the fact that I was out of breath, and managed to ram my mother down on to the

133

bed. As soon as her frail, soggy ass body hit the mattress, I was on her like a maniac landing punches and forearm strikes to her face. For a second my mother flapped around like a drowning person, flailing her hands, and trying to block my vicious licks. However, her dazed state didn't last long as she suddenly got a jolt of energy and insanity of her own. Before I knew it, my mother hand her hands in my hair, flipping me over on the mattress as she straddled me just below the waist.

"Yea you lil bitch, I got you now hoe. You don't want me to sit on your stomach and kill yo baby, do you? Fuck you and yo baby bitch after what you just did to me. Both of you bitches gonna die today!" My mother screamed like the psychopath she was as blood from her face dripped down on me and I struggled to get her off of me.

I managed to get my hands up to the head board to reach my piece of wire as my mother held my hair with one hand and pounded me in the face with the other while cursing. As soon as I felt the wire in my grip, I whipped it around my mother's neck, pulling her down closer to me, and crossing my hands with the wire ends in them at the wrist. My mother's eyes bulged out of their sockets as she felt the air in her body slowly began to leave as I tightened my grip and stared at her with hate. She reacted like a scolded dog jumping back and falling out of the bed on her stomach with me still clinging to her, but now on her back. I held the wire tightly around my mother's neck trying to squeeze the evil right out of her funky ass while for once I was the one whispering threats in someone's ear.

"Yeah hoe, who fucked up now. Your reign of terror is over mother. Who gonna save you now bitch? Where are your robots now you sick, perverted, demented BITCH! I HATE YOU! DIE!!!!!" I yelled as I continued to choke my mother with the wire and her resistance began to fade.

I could hear Sha screaming my name through the vent above my insanity but I couldn't even focus on the words he was saying. All I wanted to do at that moment was see Denise die.

"No more suffering for your sins bitch. I hope you like living in hell." I whispered in my mother's ear as I leaned in and kissed her on the head.

As soon as my lips touched her skin and I began to back away, I regretted my decision as my mother brought her head forward into my mouth and nose with so much force I fell back and blacked out for a few seconds. When I came to reality again, my mother had me by the hair as she drug me over to the bed in an attempt to tie me to it with the wire I tried to choke her with. Hearing the threat of being tied to anything was enough to light a fire under my ass so I quickly swallowed my pain and struggled to my feet. As soon as I was up, my mother and I began to exchange blow after blow like heavy weight fighters, bouncing around the room like super balls.

Sha's screams and our combined curses could be heard echoing through the air and probably the entire building as we fought like it was the end of the world. After a few minutes of back-and-forth punches and hair pulls, I was able to get some leverage over my mother by yanking her head down so that I could knee her in the face to throw her off balance. My tactic worked as my mother went crashing down to the floor and I had enough time to pull my piece of metal out of my pants. I held my mother firmly in her hair with one hand as I put my foot in her groin and used my other hand to get a good grip on the metal. I raised the metal quickly and brought it down with force before I could even think. Lucky for my mother she still had a little strength in her and was still a little quick, although crazy, because she was able to avoid the vicious blow that would have possibly sliced her head off. She squirmed under my foot and punched me in the stomach and legs as I hit her in the top of the head with the bottom of my closed fist while still holding the piece of metal.

"You evil bitch I hate you. DIE!!" I yelled as I raised the metal up high in the air again in attempt number two to slay the dragon.

I could feel anger and power surge through my body as everything seemed to slow down and I watched my arm with the metal in it glide through the air in slow motion towards my mother's neck. As soon as I began to feel the adrenaline you feel when you finally conquer a fear consume me, the pain of being hit in the back of the head and snatched by the collar of my shirt overpowered it. Before I knew what was even happening, I was being drug into the hallway like a rag doll as I watched my mother gasp for air and scrambled to get to her feet through blurred vision.

I tried to see who was pulling me by my shirt and pieces of hair that were tangled, but my vision was so blurry from the blow to the back of the head all I could see was shadows. I flapped my arms and tried to stick my hands in my pants to reach the last weapon I had tucked inside of me, but someone was quickly and firmly grabbing my hands. Suddenly, the person spoke and I knew that whatever moment of solace my brother and I had was over.

"You fucked up now princess. Look what you did to her face. Ain't shit I can do to help you right now. Naw, now yo ass gotta suffer. I told yo stupid ass to play nice. Too late now. You won't be so pretty when she's done witcha. I'm still gonna fuck you though." Duck said before kissing me deeply in the mouth and then snatching me up by the waist and throwing me over his shoulder.

I must have passed out as Duck carried me back into the room that would be my prison for months because the next thing I knew I woke up strapped to the concrete-like bed with a gag in my mouth. I felt like I would throw up as the dirty, funky tub sock Denise had in my mouth, tied around my head dipped down my throat. I struggled with my tongue trying to push the sock out as I simultaneously worked on the pieces of cloth holding my arms and feet. I struggled with all of my might, using any bit of strength I had left after the fight but no matter what I did I couldn't break free.

I finally quit struggling after a few minutes and let my head fall down on the mattress as tears fell from my eyes while I cursed and cried out in anger. I felt so overwhelmed and defeated as the pain in my body throbbed uncontrollably. I felt hysterical as I suddenly thought about my baby and wondered was he dead.

"Noooo, please let my baby be okay. Help MEEE somebody!" I screamed as I tried to break free again.

I pulled and yanked, but it was no use because I couldn't get free. I felt like I was about to hyperventilate as my heart raced and I couldn't catch my breath, imagining myself laying there with a dead baby inside of me. I think I was on the brink of insanity worrying about my baby and feeling the anxiety of being strapped to the bed until my brother made me remember that I was not alone.

"Tisha, shhh. It's okay. I'm right here sister. It's gonna be okay, Tisha." Sha said to me through his tears as I sucked up those of my own to try and comfort him.

I fought back my pain and cleared the lump in my throat as tears continued to fall from my eyes.

"I'm okay, Sha, I'm okay. You just be quiet before she remembers you're in there and comes for you. No matter what Sha remember I love you, and if you get out of here and I don't please tell someone what happened. Tell them everything, Sha, and make her pay." I said to my brother as I choked back my tears and someone began to unlock the padlocks on the door.

I glanced around quickly to see if there was anything near I could reach, but I couldn't even move my hands even if I did see something, which I didn't. Instead I just closed my eyes and let my head fall back again as I waited on the horrific fate I knew would come.

"Shhhh Sha. Don't say anything, no matter what." I whispered to my brother just as the door to my prison swung open and my mother sauntered her cracked out, sadistic voodoo doll looking ass in.

I closed my eyes, peeking out of my peripheral vision as I held my breath while watching my mother walk in with a wicker basket in her hand. I tried to make my breathing slow and labored like I was sleep but I couldn't stop my heart from racing in my chest or control my erratic breathing as that sadistic laugh of my mother's filled the air. I opened my eyes suddenly when I felt the end of the purple robe my mother was wearing brush against my face as she laid out a white towel on the bed beside me and placed a few dozen knitting needles on it. I watched with wide eyes and horror written all over my face as my mother took a candle out of the basket next and lit it before turning to stare at me. I tried to hide the fear slowly creeping up inside of me but the thought of what my mother was about to do was overwhelming.

Before I knew what had happened, I passed out, welcoming the comfort that the dark brought. Pain woke me up some time later though in the form of hot, thick needles being stuck into my thighs and the bottom of my feet. I screamed out in agony as I opened my eyes and looked directly into my mother's face. Denise showed no mercy as she continued to laugh while torturing me, sticking hot pins deep into my bruised skin.

The hot metal melted my flesh, sending electrifying pain all through my body. The pain of what was happening to me was so overpowering my mind couldn't grasp it as I suddenly went numb. I blacked out several times throughout the ordeal as my mother cursed, taunted, and spit on me while unleashing her anger. A couple of times I woke up and Duck was in the room either pleading with her to stop or passing the crack pipe and a bottle of beer. I lost consciousness several times that day and sometime in the middle of the night, I woke up with darkness all around me as Sha whispered my name.

"Tisha, wake up, you've been sleep a whole day. It's April the 26th Tisha, wake up. I think I just heard someone outside, Tisha. It sounded like Terricka. Tisha, you have to wake up. Please Tisha, don't be dead. WAKE UP!!" Sha yelled as I gained my composure enough to realize what he said.

I suddenly got the strength I needed to hold on as I listened hard against the music my mother was playing and the noise in the building to hear my big sister Terricka, yelling my name outside the little boarded up window in the room. I felt relief and hope as I yelled out for Terricka to help us and she screamed back that help was on the way. After that I let my head fall back on the mattress once again as tears of joy fell down the sides of my face. I felt happy that my sister had finally come to save us; however, something inside of me said not to cheer just yet. Something told me that I shouldn't consider myself saved too soon because we hadn't won the battle just yet.

Chapter 9

I laid there on my concrete-like bed holding my breath and anticipating the war that was about to begin as the sound of scratching on the wall next to the vent filled the air. I stretched my neck, trying to see what the noise was as it grew louder, sounding as if the entire building was about to come down. Suddenly, a loud "BOOM" like an atomic bomb filled the air and I could hear yells and curses coming from all around me. My heart raced as I thought about how my sister and her G's were invading the building and coming to rescue us from hell. The happiness I felt when I first heard my sister's voice filled my mind with hope as I stared at the door waiting for her to bust through it and pull me out. However, the nagging feeling in my heart told me that something else was on the horizon. Something inside of me was telling me to prepare for a long fight, so mentally that's what I did.

I could hear Duck and Denise scurrying down the hallway, passed my prison to their room, trying to get away from the gangstas who were inside of the building and probably up the steps, but it was no use. The next thing I heard was the sound of someone kicking the front door in followed by my sister yelling out, "Tisha, HELP IS ON THE WAY!"

"I'm in here T!" I yelled back in a hoarse voice as tears of joy rolled down my face.

I couldn't help but to release those pinned up emotions I had been carrying the past few weeks living in hell with Denise without my big sister to help me as I waited on Terricka to kick down the door. I noticed that the scratching noise in the wall had stopped just before I yelled back to tell Terricka where I was, but it was hard to decipher over all of the yells, screams, and footsteps in the hallway. Denise's curses filled the air as I heard her run back passed the room with Duck following her. Seconds later Terricka had her ear on the door calling my name as she tried to push and kick it in.

"Tish, you okay? What the fuck happened? How did you get here? Where is Sha, Tisha?" Terricka yelled over all of the mayhem in the hallway as my emotions got the best of me.

I don't know why I felt so overwhelmed at that moment, maybe it was because I was so relieved to hear my sister's voice or I was just anxious to be free. Whatever the reason was I couldn't control myself as I cried and screamed, trying to answer Terricka's questions through the thick door and my muffled sobbing voice.

"I DUNNO Whhha Happened TERRICKA. I don't know where Sha at…. I can't breathe T. Help me!" I said to my sister as I felt one of my panic attack, catatonic episodes coming on.

My heart raced so fast in my chest it felt as if a sack of a million bees were living behind my breasts. I couldn't stop my body from trembling as I held on to the pieces of cloth and wire holding me to the bed posts, trying to calm the panic growing inside of me.

"I can't breathe, Terricka. I don't know what happened. She came and she took us. Sha …he was in the closet next door but now I don't know. Terricka help!" I yelled as my sister pounded on the door and yelled for someone to help her, but muffled yells and far-off cries of men all around the apartment quickly told us no help was around.

I tried hard to swallow down the spit in my mouth and the lump in my throat as my heart continued to race, yet there was no use. My body shook uncontrollably, and the room began to spin like I was on the tea cup ride from hell. The shakes and waves of anxiety consuming my body at that moment were so intense, I couldn't control any of my body's functions. I felt like my body was falling apart as my sister tried tirelessly to get inside the room before running over to the closet, trying to get in there as well. I heard her yell for Sha followed by his faint moan then Terricka was back at my door.

"Tisha, what the fuck is these doors made of? Steel? I can't get in there without help. I'm fina go get somebody to help me and I'll be right back!" Terricka yelled as she ran down the hall and I felt like I was drowning in an ocean of water.

I felt frantic as my only lifeline began to slowly slip away. I didn't want my sister to leave me, not even for a moment after she had left me alone for so long.

"NO TERRICKA PLEASE DON'T GO! PLLEEASE!" I yelled as I struggled against my restraints, using the little supply of air I had left.

I felt my lungs began to contract, but barely release as my mind reeled and I continued to struggle against the restraints that held my wrists. I only began to slowly relax when I heard Terricka's footsteps as she returned to the door to comfort me.

"Shhh Tisha, calm down. I'm right here. I'll never leave you if I can help it. You have to calm down though. I heard you're pregnant too, damn sis. Jerrod gonna be so happy when he finds out." My sister said as my calmness began to disappear and panic crept back in.

Hearing Jerrod's name sent me into hysterics because for weeks I'd expected the worse only for my sister to casually mention him like he was around the corner. I hoped that meant he was okay and Terricka had seen him. I could barely get the words out as I cry hiccoughed and tried to catch my breath.

"Where is he, Terricka? I need him, where is he? I can't breathe." I said to my sister as everything began to get dim.

I felt like I was falling down a black hole as my body began to shake again and I tried to listen to Terricka's voice as she yelled through the door. After a few minutes of uncontrollable shaking, I could finally make sense of her words again as she calmed the fear inside of me.

"SHARTISHA, PLEASE LISTEN TO ME! You are okay little sister. Jerrod is okay too. I don't know exactly where he at or when he coming back, but sis you have to trust me when I say he aite. You gotta calm down and focus on yourself and that baby. I'm gonna get you out of there, but you have to calm down first. Listen to me, Tisha. Listen to our Salvation song." My sister said as the room came back into focus and I could concentrate on my breathing.

Soon the melodic sound of my sister's voice filled the air as the words to our Salvation Song soothed my soul. I couldn't help but drop a few more tears as I sang along with my sister like I'd done many times before.

"Nothing is forever, what we're hoping for,

No more pain so don't you cry anymore.

Hold your head up high and dry yo tears,

Let me help you through and erase yo fears.

We'll overcome it all, if we stick together,

We just gotta believe that nothing lasts forever (nothing lasts forever)."

My sister and I both sang through the six inch thick steel door.

I listened to my sister while slightly sobbing and breathing hard through the door for a few seconds as I gathered my emotions and put them in my back pocket. I tried to forget about all of the pain and heartache unless it was to channel the anger I needed to survive. I remembered everything my sister had told me through my haze as I sucked up my tears and called out for her.

"Terricka. I'm alright now. Get me out of here though. This shit cutting off my circulation. Terricka, TERRICKA!" I yelled as I waited on my sister to respond.

All that I could hear in the hallway outside my room at that moment was muted footsteps and the muffled sounds of a struggle. Suddenly the voice of the devil poured through the thick steel and sent chills straight to my spine.

"You little funky bitch. I knew I'd get my hands on yo ass again. I'm gonna kill you hoe!" I heard Denise yell out as Terricka's muffled cry followed.

I could tell from the sounds that my mother and Terricka were tussling and that more than likely Denise was choking my sister, which is why I could barely hear her voice. Suddenly, there was a loud impact on the door as someone was slammed into it.

"Yeah bitch, you was looking for me Denise, huh? Well, here I am you funky, maggot ass junky hoe. I hate you, sick bitch. You ain't shit to me. Die hoe! I'll stomp yo fucking head in!" My sister yelled as I heard Denise crying out in agony and something hard hit against the bottom of the door repeatedly.

The next thing I heard was the faint sound of a small caliber gun being shot followed by my sister yelling and her fleeing footsteps. I cried to the top of my lungs as my heart went crazy in my chest and I imagined my sister being shot. I could do nothing but cry, shake, and scream Terricka's name as I heard Duck ask my mother if she was okay on the other side of the door. I knew right then it was him that had come to my mother's rescue and possibly killed my sister in the process. I made it up in my mind at that moment that I would make his bitch ass pay for that.

"TERRICKA! SHATERRICKA, answer me please!" I cried, waiting for my sister to reply.

I held my breath and bit my bottom lip, waiting to hear Terricka's voice, a whimper, anything. However, I was met by the ugly, evil voice of the savage from my nightmares. My mother growled and huffed behind the door like a deranged beast as I stared at the steel door that separated us, hoping she wouldn't come in.

"Don't call for her, she fucked up. While you worrying about her though, you better worry about yourself and that little mute. It's gonna be three dead bitches before today over with. Mark my words, Tisha, I'll be back." My mother threatened before I heard her footsteps trail off down the hall.

I laid there silent for a moment, just listening, because I had the feeling that someone was still around. When I finally heard Duck laugh from the other side, I knew my instinct was right, someone was lurking.

"Y'all lil bitches something else, some real spitfires I tell you that. But yo sister fucked up. That lil bitch stabbed me so she gotta die. Fat's lil bitch, trader ass too. Don't you worry though princess, I'll keep you safe, and your brother too. All you have to do is be nice to me, remember? Anyway, let me get back to it. See you after this business is over." Duck said laughing as he ran off down the hall.

I exhaled deeply, releasing the pinned up tension I had inside as I yelled my sister's name over and over again while screams, furniture breaking, and gunshots rang out in the house and apartments around us. I felt like my head was about to explode from screaming so loud and hard when I suddenly heard the scratching and scraping noise in the wall begin again. I quickly turned my head and squinted my eyes, trying to see who or what was coming through the vent.

All of a sudden the vent cover and a piece of the wall on both sides of the vent came crashing down to the floor and a dusty, wild looking Sha fell through grinning. I couldn't help but to smile too as my brother jumped to his feet and ran over to the bed to untie me. I sighed in relief as Sha released my outstretched arms and legs, giving me some much needed relief. I had to lay there for a few minutes in the fetal position until my limbs stopped throbbing. However, as soon as the pain subsided I was on my feet trying to find a way out.

"Sha didn't you hear Terricka talking to you earlier? She's in here you know? We gotta get out of here. How did you get that vent open?" I asked Sha as I bent down and measured the vent space with my eyes.

I quickly concluded that I would be able to get through it without hurting myself after a short inspection and turned to face Sha before suggesting we go back through the vent. I figured we'd have a better chance getting out the closet door than the steel door of the room we were in. I stared at Sha and waited on his response before darting over to the bed to get my stick Denise had left in the room after our fight. She had taken my piece of metal and used my piece of wire to bind me; however, there was two weapons she didn't get. She didn't get the piece of wood I held in my hand or the pocket knife I kept tucked deep inside. I had left placed that knife inside of me every day since I found it just waiting until I needed it most. I could feel that time was coming as I stared at my dingy brother.

"I heard her, Tisha, but I was in the vents. Most of the vents in this house are connected. That could be our way out. The one on the opposite side of the closet leads to the hallway. We could find Terricka. Let's go, Tish." Sha said crawling back into the vent as I followed with my stick in hand.

The squeeze into the vent was a little more snug than I anticipated as I twisted and turned my body until I made it through. Once inside the small, dark, stinky, cramped closet, Sha led me straight to the other vent, stopping just before he climbed inside.

"Okay Tisha, this one is about the same size as the last one with a sharp left turn just ahead. When you get up there, turn your head left as you go in and keep turning your body left along with it, you'll make it through. Now follow me." Sha said as he began going through the vent.

Halfway inside my brother stopped and turned back to look at me as I crouched down with the stick in my hand.

"On second thought, Tisha, I think you should go first. That way if you get stuck I can push you from behind." Sha said coming back out of the vent and pulling me forward.

I crawled into the vent and realized that what my brother said was true. That vent was pretty much the same size as the other with an exception of the sharp turn. When I got to it, I tried turning my head easily to the left and letting the rest of my body glide along through the vent like Sha had said. However, when I did that shit nothing went as planned. My head and neck went through fine, but when it got to my shoulders and turning my abdomen straight to come through, pain shot up my body like electricity. I tried to cover my mouth with my hand to muffle my screams as my legs and feet cramped up and my shoulders got lodged in the turn.

Before the panic that was brewing in my stomach could kick in to full capacity, Sha was at my feet massaging them and my legs as he calmed me down.

"Shhh, Tisha, you're okay. I've done this a dozen time in the past two days. You'll be fine just do a slow wiggle like a fish out of water while moving your head to the left. As you do that, push off of my hands and I will help guide you forward." Sha said as I did everything he told me to do. Suddenly I bust head first through the open vent into the hall way.

I fell on to my side and quickly jumped to my feet, pressing my body into the wall trying to blend into the darkness. I could hear someone hollering right outside of the building as I helped Sha up to his feet while keeping my eyes trained on the doorway to the hall.

"Follow me Sha and stay close." I whispered to my brother through the darkness as we stealth down the hallway towards the living room and the front door.

I held my breath at the doorway before summoning the courage to peek inside. When I looked into the living room, I was shocked by what I saw. The entire room was in shambles from what I could see through the darkness and blood was everywhere. A man I recognized to be Duck's friend was laying by the door with gashes, wounds, knots, and cuts all over him. I gasped as I crept closer and noticed that his face had been beaten so severely you couldn't even see where his eyes were. I pushed Sha behind me as I stepped over the man's body and he moaned while pee poured from between his legs and formed a puddle beneath him.

My legs trembled as I made it passed the man with Sha behind me and approached the open front door. I swallowed hard and encouraged myself as I got a good grip on my stick and prepared to fight. I stepped forward with Sha almost attached at my hip, and peered out into the hallway to see my sister wrapped in a vicious fight with my mother. Terricka had my mother by the hair, smashing her in the face with her fist as my mother delivered punch after punch to my sister's head. I quickly glanced around to see if anyone else was in the hall before turning to tell Sha to stay put.

As soon as the words left my mouth, I dashed out of the door and ran at my mother and sister like a runaway freight train. I hit my mother with force using the stick in my hand as the nails penetrated her back and she let go of her grip on my sister's hair. Denise fell to the floor hard like a 100 year old oak tree as my sister and I commenced to beating her ass like a runaway slave.

I stomped my mother repeatedly in the head and back as Terricka punched her in the face and cursed, remembering every single thing she had ever done to us. I couldn't control my rage as I straddled my mother's back and put her in a head lock, choking her until I felt her body get weak. Suddenly as I choked my mother and Terricka punched her over and over in the face, Sha's frantic voice filled the air consuming my heart with fear.

I slowly turned my head to look at my brother and find out what was so important when I was met suddenly by something hard and forceful. The impact from whatever hit me in my face was so powerful I felt my body glide across the hallway and hit the wall as Terricka yelled out my name. The next thing I saw was momentary darkness followed by flashes of my mother kicking me in the face and then hearing her yell for Duck to call the police and tell them that Terricka and Fat had done everything. I passed out after that and only woke up again when Duck threw me across his shoulder and carried me out of the hall. I tried to open my eyes to see where I was being taken as Duck told someone that Terricka and Fat were hiding in the building. However, the blood and tears on my eyes was so crusty I couldn't open them. All I could do was beg Duck to put me down and let me go.

"Please Duck let me go. Where is my brother, where's Terricka? Please let me and my baby go. Please." I pleaded with Duck as he continued to walk slowly and quietly like an undertaker with a new body.

I struggled in his arms as I felt him take me inside somewhere cramped, and stinky. I quickly recognized the smell as that of the closet Sha was kept in and felt some relief knowing that at least I would be with my brother. However, when I felt Duck throw me down to the floor and heard a board in the closet move, I knew things were different. Suddenly, I was being flung into an even smaller and darker space as Sha moaned out in pain from my body being thrust on top of his. I quickly moved slightly to the side and ground the dried blood out of my eyes to see. When I was able to focus and look around the tiny space, I gasped in horror. Someone had cut a small two by four foot hole in the wall and fixed a bar on the outside, in which they locked me and Sha in like we were animals. I cringed as Duck slammed the metal bars closed and pressed his ugly, perverse ass face up against it.

"Damn princess, you fucked up now. Ain't shit I can to do help none of y'all. Your sister good as dead if her ass don't go to jail first. Y'all fucked your mama up good. She on the way to the hospital so I'ma deal with you later. Sweet dreams." Duck said laughing as he threw a can with thick white fog coming out of it into the cage.

I spit in his face as the smoke started filling the tiny space and I watched through blurred vision as he wiped my spit off with his finger before licking it. I began to cough uncontrollably as I pressed my body up against Sha's while pulling my shirt up over my nose and mouth while instructing my brother to do the same. The chemicals in the fog burned my lungs, skin, eyes, and throat as I gasped for air and cradled my brother, trying to take the brunt of the punishment. Duck laughed at us huddled together as he put the piece of plaster that hid the cage back in place and left the closet.

I breathed some of the fresh air that was still in my lungs into my brother's mouth as he turned purple and began to go unconscious. I tried to fight the effects of the chemicals for as long as I could; however, as I held Sha's head in my hands and called his name, I knew I was in a never winning battle. The last thing I remember before darkness took me again was hearing the muffled voices of police officers as they entered the apartment, after that I was gone.

Chapter 10

    I woke up the next day, April 27th, tied to the headboard with wire again as someone moaned in the darkness while sitting on the bed next to me. I squinted my eyes and stared at the back of a nappy head, which I quickly recognized as Duck as he moved his arm up and down quickly. I couldn't see exactly what he was doing through the thick darkness in the room; however, the way he was moaning and moving his body told me that he was being nasty as fuck. I instantly felt flustered like I would pass out or hyperventilate as I squirmed in the bed and tried to pull my arms out of the wrapped wire that was cutting into my wrists. The realization that I couldn't get out was apparent as blood began to trickle down my arms from the gashes I had formed trying to free my hands from the wire. I cried out in pain as the wounds throbbed and the wire continued to dig into the gashes.

    "Ahhh, Duck please, let me go. Undo my wrists. It's hurting and I'm bleeding. Help me." I cried as warm blood continued to run down my arms and into my armpits.

I waited on Duck's response as pain and anxiety surged through me and I peered around the room beyond the darkness just looking for something. I was looking for anything I could use to fuck up the pedophile sitting inches away from me, but of course nothing was within my reach. I held my breath as Duck slowly turned around towards me, bringing his face so close to mine I could smell the Burnette's Vodka he had been drinking.

I swallowed down the vomit that was creeping up my throat as Duck laughed and stared at me with those pop eyes, drinking me in as he turned to reveal himself to me. I quickly closed my eyes and bit my bottom lip, fuming and filled with fear over what I knew was about to happen. I tried to calm the rage burning inside of me that was derived from my fear, but there was no use. I yelled curses at Duck for sitting there staring at me with his dick in his hand like a real, *To Catch a Predator*, instead of helping me. I wanted to head butt him and knock his fucking teeth out as he laughed at my anger, treating me like a piece of shit.

"You sick ass bitch help me. What the fuck wrong with you. HELP ME!" I yelled through clenched teeth as I struggled against the wires lifting my torso up off the bed before trying to bite Duck's nose off.

I almost had his slimy ass too, but the crack he had been smoking made him quick so he was able to jump back in time.

"Ohhh, princess. Now you fucking up like yo lil hoe ass sister. Y'all lil bitches really think y'all bad, huh? Well, we will see how bad that lil nappy head bitch is locked up in jail for the next six to eight months." Duck said as I gasped and growled before cursing and spitting at him.

"You muthafucka. I hate you too. You bastard!" I screamed through my tears as I thought about my sister locked up, alone in an adult facility.

I went crazy in the bed flapping my body around, trying to kick and punch at him but the wires barely allowed me to move. All that I could do was scream to the top of my lungs and curse my tormentor.

"SHUT THE FUCK UP!" Duck yelled in a deep, sadistic tone that made my insides quiver.

I quickly shut my mouth, biting my lip while crying and imagining the day I could fuck him up.

I held my breath and closed my eyes as Duck laughed and used the index finger of his left hand to trace the curves of my body. I opened my eyes and stared at his face as he wore this far off, almost drugged out expression, while running his finger just below my breast. I cringed when his rough, callused skin touched me, causing goosebumps to pop up all over my body. I silently prayed and wished someone could help me as thoughts of what would take place ran through my mind.

In that moment I knew that the turmoil of my past would surely continue. I knew right then that the peace I had gained living with the Robinson's was gone. Once again my body would not be my own. I would have to barter my health, sanity, and life for my innocence. I felt defeated, but angry as fuck knowing that like countless times before I was going to have to wager the only piece of the world that was truly my own. I felt my heart break into a million pieces as Duck continued to laugh while tracing my body back down to my honey pot, rubbing it lightly.

"Stop all that damn yelling, Tisha. I'm done fucking with you. I tried being nice to yo funky ass and giving you an opportunity to play the game the nice way, but you didn't want that, did you? The nice way would have allowed you and your brother luxuries Denise would never approve, if you were nice to me. Now that doesn't sound like such a bad plan considering all the shit yo mammy crazy ass do and has done to you. I was gonna make it so there was only one nigga you fucked and sucked on a regular, ME! I was gonna take care of yo silly ass girl." Duck said rubbing his face up and down the side of mine.

"You fucked that up though." He said breathing hard like an overweight stripper on stage for three songs before kissing me in the corner of my mouth.

The smell of Duck's breath and just having him touching me, reminding me of my first monster Jerome, was too much for my little pregnant belly to handle. Before I knew it, I was puking up the little food in my stomach as Duck jumped up looking on with a smile on his face. I choked on my own vomit for a second before turning my head and allowing it to flow to the side instead of back up into my face. Once I caught my breath and was able to get all of the boiling contents of my stomach up, I glared at Duck through watery eyes.

If looks could kill, I am sure he would have been dead at that second. I stared at that bastard with all of the pain and hurt I had for everyone who had ever abused or used me, wishing from my heart that God really would strike people down. I wished something would happen to his demented ass. I needed a miracle, something like a divine intervention that would save me from another degrading act. That was my wish, but wishes just like luck didn't apply to me or any of my siblings. All that we got from the world was heartache, pain, and a reminder that we were cursed for ever being born. What Duck did next proved that.

"Awww, the princess not feeling good, huh? Ha! Good you got all that shit out of yo stomach already because now we about to play my game. All that easy way shit out the window, Tisha. I got you here and I'm about to do what the fuck ever I want to." Duck said as he ripped the shirt I had on down the middle revealing my engorged, perky DD breasts.

I felt so disgusted, worthless, and just down right low as Duck admired my breasts and I begged him to just leave me alone for my baby's sake. As he stepped up to me with his penis in his hand, I knew that there was no reasoning with him. Tears ran down the sides of my face as I cried out of anger huffing and biting my lip the entire time.

"Alright now princess let's get this straight now. I know this isn't an ideal situation for getting or giving some head, BUT you leave me no choice. SO if YOU, bite, nip, or even scrape my dick I will beat you to death with my bare hands then cut that bastard out of yo stomach and beat him to death too. DO you understand?" Duck asked through clenched teeth with a sadistic expression on his face before quickly standing up straight while smiling.

I shook my head yes that I understood as my tears continued to flow and I watched the black version of *American Psycho* prepare to put his penis in my mouth. At that moment I could hear my sister's voice in my head telling me to be strong and to sing our song. I tucked my lips, closed my eyes, and blocked out the feelings consuming me, focusing on the words of the song as Duck walked over to the bed. I watched as he clicked on the lamp next to the bed before letting his pants fall down to the floor. I barely had time to squint my eyes in an effort to adjust them to the light before quickly jumping on the bed, straddling my face. The smell of Duck's groin was poignant and rank as he waved his pink, spotty, five inch organ in my face. The stench was so bad that my eyes watered and I dry heaved in my mouth as he grabbed me in the back of my hair.

"Now remember what I said Princess, suck it like a Popsicle. Oh my bad. I don't have to tell you, you're a pro. Now open yo MUTHAFUCKING mouth and go for what you know HOE!" Duck Said through clenched teeth as he grabbed my jaw, prying it open with his fingers as I cried and mentally hummed the Salvation Song.

Before Duck's dirty, stinky penis could even touch my tongue, the relief the Salvation Song offered had helped me to transcend out of my body once again. I felt numb as I laid there bound by my wrists and ankles as Duck thrust up and down in my mouth gagging me while pulling my hair. Tears ran down the side of my face as he held my hair in both hands and jerked my head back and forth like a madman. I felt nothing when he reached back and grabbed my breasts pinching and turning them like they were handles on a faucet.

The only time I felt anything, coming back to the moment and feeling everything that was happening, was when he touched my stomach. As soon as I felt his evil touch on my precious gift, electricity shot through my body and I began flapping around wildly. In the process of flapping I nipped the tip of Duck's dick and he quickly slapped me hard across the face as a punishment. I glared at him while biting my lip as he jerked my hair, pulling my face towards him.

"Bitch didn't I say I'd kill you if you bit me? I will touch whatever I want to on you and don't you forget that. I got something for yo ass." Duck said as he wrapped his hand around my throat and went so far down my throat that he made my uvula touch the top of my esophagus.

I gagged and squirmed as Duck continued to thrust down my throat while reaching back and rubbing my stomach in a circular motion. Soon he was thrusting quickly in my mouth and holding my hair again before exploding all over my face. I closed my eyes and held my breath as the hot, sticky liquid ran down my eye and into my hairline. I felt like something lower than dirt as he smiled down at me and then smeared his semen all over my face. I laid there livid, frozen in anger as I watched Duck casually get up off the bed, unpinning my sore, outstretched arms and grabbing his dirty, shitty underwear off the ground. As he put them on, I glared at him while my tears mixed with his juices still left on my face, and I vowed to make him pay with his blood. No matter what it took I was going to make Duck's nasty ass regret the day he ever met me.

"Death is too good for you bitch, but I got something for ya." I said to myself as I continued to watch the pedophile dress through hateful eyes.

"What you say, Tisha? Don't mumble, say what you have to say out loud. Remember who in control here sweetheart. Now, thank you for giving me some of the best head I've ever had, a bit sloppy but great nonetheless. Now, you get some sleep because I got a feeling this good review I'm about to give you will have the niggas knocking this door down." Duck said as he wiped my face with the dirty, damp towel he had sitting on the dresser and then kissed me on the forehead before laughing.

I did nothing but glare at Duck as he laughed his way to the door, swinging it open just as my mother walked back into the house and down the hall. The light from the hallway illuminated the other dark half of the room making it possible for me to clearly see my mother's face. When our eyes met, the hate was so strong smoke seemed to come from her eyeballs as she stared me down.

"You little bitch, I'm gonna fuck you up. I promise you that!" Denise yelled as she lunged forward with a bandage wrapped around her head, one on her face, and one on her left hand.

I kind of smirked as I watched her try to get passed Duck to put her hands on me looking like a ghetto mummy for Halloween that only had a half of roll of tissue. My laughter infuriated her so much I could see steam coming out of her ears as she growled and threatened me while Duck held her back.

"Oh you little slut bag bitch! You think it's funny? I'm gonna fuck you up cunt just wait!" My mother yelled pushing Duck back into the room as she tried harder to get me.

"DENISE..STOOOPPP. Killing her ain't gonna benefit us. Now, that mouth is fantastic. That's what you need to focus on, finding some customers for that cap." Duck said calming my mother as I watched the wheels in her brain start to move slowly like an obese hamster on one of those exercise wheels.

I could see revenge flare in her eyes as she smirked at me retreating from her mission of beating my ass. Instead she backed out of the room with her arms in the air, smiling at me and letting me know that more hurt was to come. If I could have predicted the pain, I would go through over the six months following that day I probably would have begged her to kill me right then, but I couldn't. Instead I just laid there crying as my mother stared at me, creating a plan in her mind that would seal the deal on my six months of torture.

"You right Duck. I ain't gonna kill the bitch, but after all the muthafuckas I send in here to tear her mouth and ass out she will wish her ass was dead. I'm gonna show you wanch, not to fuck with me. Bitch gonna get my money, just watch." My mother said before laughing again as I closed my eyes and turned my head.

I pretended that my mother and Duck weren't still standing there in the door kissing and laughing at me as I thought about how sweet my revenge would be when it finally came.

"Hard times don't last always. Look forward to the rainbow after the storm." Echoed in my mind as I imagined my uncle Scooby's face as while he said that to me.

Those words helped me through that night by providing me with a source of strength to block out the pain. I used it when my mother came into the room a couple of hours later and stuck lit cigarettes to my flesh. I used it again in the middle of the night when Duck snuck back in and spent an hour with his face buried between my legs as I cried and tried to make myself invisible. Those words helped me through the days and weeks to come; however, as the list of men and boys my mother sent into the room to violate me grew longer, those words proved less effective. I laid there tied to that bed for days on end before anyone let me up, only seeing people when someone was coming to fondle me or relieve themselves in my mouth.

Duck brought us food and Sha and I talked and prayed through the vent daily, but other than that I just laid there and cried. After being tied to the bed for an entire month, Duck allowed his niece, who was an OB nurse to come over and check me and the baby out. She examined us while looking at me like I was an alien or some shit as if she wasn't the fucked up person who came to examine and treat a 17-year-old pregnant girl who was strapped to a bed. I couldn't believe the audacity of that ratchette hoe as she rolled her eyes at me and popped her gum while taking my vitals. After getting a clean bill of health and enough prenatal vitamins to last the rest of my pregnancy, I was locked back in my prison alone with nothing but my brother's voice to keep me going.

The months I was locked away in that room, chained to that bed seemed to go by at a turtle's pace. I watched myself get bigger and bigger as I laid on my back and stared up at the ceiling of my prison. My pregnancy was miserable because my back hurt all of the time and my limbs were sore from being tied up 85% of the time. Aside from that I was being violated like clockwork almost 20 times a week as guy after guy came through that steel door with their dick in their hands and left with a piece of my soul.

I was able to finesse most of them out of having sex with me, even if they paid for it by talking about the baby moving and growing inside of my stomach. The majority of the guys would feel awkward and just take the blow job and leave. Some of them would refuse to touch me at all and just sit and talk for their time. I was relieved those times and kind of looked at those guys as less dangerous, but still sadistic bastards. However, all of them were sick as fuck for not reporting what was happening to me.

My luck of finessing the tricks ran out though on October 18th right after I had just turned eight months pregnant. I remember that day like it was yesterday because it was the worst day of my fucking life. Duck had just finished feeding me hamburger helper and cornbread as I laid tied to the bed when my mother walked in with this fat, greasy, black man with overalls on. He had gold and diamond chains and rings on every finger and big diamond earrings that sparkled in the hall light. He was like a great big Christmas bulb all sparkly and shit, standing there grinning at me with that familiar pedophile glance. After a short introduction, I found out he was a big dope boy from Mississippi my mother was trying to impress so I was told to be on my best behavior.

I sucked up my anger and hurt as I closed my eyes and prepared to put the fat man's tiny penis in my mouth. However, when I felt him raise the gown I was wearing that day and began to sick his fingers inside of me, panic surged through me fast. I didn't want his fingers inside of me violating my baby and I also didn't want him to find the switchblade I had stuffed up there for good keeping. I knew that I had to do something to get his attention away from my lower half and get him up to my mouth which was the only real weapon I had left with my limbs always being bound. I thought fast on my feet as I remembered some of the lines Lisa used to tell me and my sister Terricka from when she was a stripper. I quickly adapted one of the most memorable skits I saw her do, making it fit my circumstance and bait the fat fucker in.

"Ohh daddy. That pussy not wet yet but this mouth is. Come put that big dick in my mouth. If you do that this monkey will get wet." I said to the fat man in my best seductive voice as he grinned while still sticking his finger inside of me.

For a second I thought he felt the knife inside of me as he stopped moving his hand and stared at my face. However, after he suddenly grabbed himself and hurried up to my mouth, I knew that the warmth and moisture from inside of me had just excited him and I had him right where I needed him to be.

"Yea come on and put it in yo mouth you lil nasty pregnant bitch. I heard about you. They say you ain't had no head until lil Denise give it to you. I can't wait to feel it. Then I'ma fuck you to death, long and hard whether you want it or not." The fat, pedophile creep said as I felt the anger inside of me ignite.

"What the fuck did you just say?" I asked him through clenched teeth as he laughed and rubbed his penis on my lips.

Hearing him say I was considered to be a mini version of my mother made me so mad I saw red as I let him put his baby penis in my mouth. All I could do was think about those words as I closed my eyes and sucked the tiny tic tac between my lips. The fat man moaned and closed his eyes, holding his head back and moaning as I deep throated his tiny dick while playing with his balls. I smiled as I looked up at him in ecstasy with his head back. He was really enjoying his blow job at that moment and I was enjoying the thought of fucking him up as I took his penis out of my mouth and licked his balls. I put both of his testicles into my mouth despite my urge to throw up, all because I wanted desperately to get revenge. I was going to show him who was a mini Denise if I didn't do anything else.

Just as I felt his dick grow to its capacity and he was about to blow, I bit down on his nuts as hard as I could, cutting through his flesh like a hot knife through butter. I locked on his balls like a pit bull, shaking and pulling them until I had completely bitten one off. The slow drawling cry of the man suddenly filled the air as he screamed like hot coal was up his ass. I smirked at him as he looked down at me and covered the spot his balls used to be in with his hands.

I smirked as I watched him run to the door and try to get out, but Denise had locked it from the outside. He stood there with wide eyes, screaming until Denise finally opened the door and he burst out like a bat out of hell. Shock, anger, and a hint of pride was written all over Denise's face as she stood there in the doorway glaring at me. I spit the balls I held in my mouth towards her and watched as it landed at her feet.

"Now you happy bitch. That's what gonna happen to every other muthafucka you send in here. You hear me bitch?" I yelled at my mother as sparks of rage danced in her eyes.

I cringed as she lunged towards me, grabbing my hair and yanking my head to the side just as Duck bust in the room to intervene.

"WHOOOAAHH, what's going on in here Denise? What the fuck happened to Big Terry? He running through this bitch like his ass on fire." Duck asked as he held Denise and I looked at him smirking with blood running down my mouth.

My mother quickly filled Duck in on what happened as I laid there laughing, feeling satisfied that I was finally making muthafuckas feel the pain that I felt. My laughter turned to slight fear as my mother agreed to go after the fat man and Duck stayed there with me. He smiled at me with that nasty, sneaky smile as he closed the door and walked deep into the room. My heart raced as I watched him begin to peel the layers of clothing he had on before walking over to the bed.

"Tonight gonna be special princess., for ME and YOU. I ain't none of fat man so you can try that shit if you want to and get the shit beat out of you. It's best just to play nice with your fine ass. That belly getting bigger and I know that pussy is soo warm and wet. I have to get me some of it before you drop that rugrat. Ain't no way I'm gonna wait six weeks to feel this. Now, I'm gonna untie your arms for this because I want you to hold me, but don't try nothing or I will fuck you up Tisha." Duck said as he leaned over and unwound the wire that held my wrists to the headboard.

I felt nothing but relief as he released my arms letting them fall down to the bed. As soon as I had my arms stretched out ready to help me attack my mind went to the switchblade stuck up my snatch. I knew that I had to get it out so that I could fuck Duck up, but with him standing over me butt naked and dick in hand, I didn't see how it would be possible. Just then I heard my brother bang the wall inside the vents diverting Duck's attention away.

"You better go check that Duck. It may be the police after how that fat bitch ran up out of

184

here." I said to Duck as I watched his stupid ass consider what I was saying.

Before I could even be in disbelief at how dumb he was he had darted out of the room and I had my hand up my vagina, pulling the switchblade out. I quickly tucked it under my thigh just as Duck bust back into the room smiling and telling me everything was fine. As soon as the words had left his mouth, Duck was back on top of me in the bed, wedging himself in between my legs and penetrating my semi-wet vagina. I cried out in pain and despair as Duck dug deep inside of me and moaned while pulling my hair. I stared up into his face as I took the knife out from under my leg, opened it, and held it firmly. I tried to stop the anger from surging through my body as I thought about where to stick Duck first, but my fury was so strong I couldn't think straight. As he got leverage inside of me using the bed, while wrapping his hand around my throat, I had enough.

It was like time slowed down and someone or something invaded my body as I raised my hand quickly and precisely, stabbing Duck 15 times in the stomach before he could even blink his eye. Each time I stabbed him, I turned the knife opening the wound and ripping the flesh and organs inside. Duck jumped up off of me screaming and running like a scalded dog, quite similar to the pedophile before him as I laughed and immediately went to work cutting undoing the wires on my legs.

I watched him run out of the room and leave the door open as I continued to work on releasing my legs. Within minutes I was up and on my feet feeling wobbly from the 100 extra pounds I was carrying and the stress of all I had gone through. Laying down for the most part of six months hadn't helped any ether as my legs felt like jello underneath me. I didn't care about any of that though as I made my way to the door and ran straight to the closet next door. I flung it open quick and expected to grab my brother up and escape; however, all I found was an empty closet when I opened the unlocked door.

"Sha, Sha where are you?" I whispered as I crawled into the closet and put my face near the vent. I could hear something moving around in the walls and I knew it was Sha; however, I couldn't figure out where he was. All I could do was call his name.

"Sha come out, let's go." I said as I suddenly heard footsteps coming down the hall behind me.

I quickly pushed my large body into the opening of the open vent and pulled the cover back over it as my mother opened the closet door screaming my brother's name.

"Shamel, you retarded bastard, where are you? I'm fucking y'all up. I'm done playing. Where you at fucker?" Densie yelled as I held my mouth with my hands, keeping my screams inside.

After a few seconds of looking around the tiny closet and screaming, my mother left the room and walked to her bedroom. As soon as I heard her going down that end of the hall, I dashed out of the vent, into the closet, and out into the hall. I waited until I saw my mother open her bedroom door and step in before I dashed out of the closet and into the living room, straight towards the front door. Just as I touched the knob I heard a blood curdling scream come from my mother's room, followed by her calling Duck's name. I knew right then she had

187

found him and saw that I fucked up two people she sent to destroy me in one night.

I felt slightly victorious as I unlocked the front door, leaving it open while whispering Sha's name. I was going to find my brother and escape hell, never to see my mother again. That was the plan I had in my mind. However, when I heard my mother yell my name in an evil voice before cocking her gun, I knew that things wouldn't work out as I planned. I bolted out of the apartment as fast as I could in the Mickey Mouse gown Duck had put me in days before and my bare feet. I went down the stairs slowly and methodically, trying not to fall as my legs wobbled and my hands shook on the rail. I could hear my mother coming as I continued to go down the stairs and she yelled my name from up above.

"Tisha you bitch. I hate you. You killed Duck. You take something from me and I'll take something from you bitch. Say goodbye to this retard." My mother yelled as I looked up to see her dangling my brother's unconscious body over the railing.

Time slowed again as I yelled for her to stop and told her I would do whatever she wanted while running back up the steps. I felt like I was running in quicksand as I tried to make it back to the top of the stairwell to save my brother. I got up five steps up before my mother did the unthinkable, destroying a part of me I could never get back. I watched from outside of myself as my brother's limp body went soaring over the stairwell, three stories down to the ground. When Sha's body hit the bottom, it made a loud thud as his head split open like a watermelon. I remember looking up into my mother's hateful eyes before everything went back and I fell backwards down the concrete steps, ready to meet the same fate as my brother.

CPSIA information can be obtained
at www.ICGtesting.com
Printed in the USA
LVHW012322250720
661537LV00021B/2339